A Candlelight Ecstasy Romance™

SHE WAS RACING ALONG A BEACH BESIDE AN ENDLESS SEA. . . .

She was running so fast, she seemed to be flying, her feet hardly touching the ground as she dodged the lacy foam. Breathlessly she sensed the approach of the man who was pursuing her, and her heart thumped wildly with expectation.

Then suddenly the scene shifted. She was in a roofless cave, submerged in the warmth of her lover's arms, drowning in the excitement of his kiss. But when she tried to look into his face, she awoke, terribly, frighteningly alone. Was it a beautiful dream or an ecstatic memory? Would she ever see that face? Recall his name? Would she ever find the man who possessed her past and haunted her dreams?

CANDLELIGHT ECSTASY ROMANCES™

Promises
to Keep

Rose Marie Ferris

A CANDLELIGHT ECSTASY ROMANCE™

Published by
Dell Publishing Co., Inc.
1 Dag Hammarskjold Plaza
New York, New York 10017

Dell ® TM 681510, Dell Publishing Co., Inc.

Candlelight Ecstasy Romance™ is a trademark of
Dell Publishing Co., Inc., New York, New York.

ISBN: 0–440–17159–8

Printed in the United States of America

First printing—November 1981

Dear Reader:

In response to your enthusiasm for Candlelight Ecstasy Romances™, we are now increasing the number of titles per month from two to three.

We are pleased to offer you sensuous novels set in America, depicting modern American women and men as they confront the provocative problems of a modern relationship.

Throughout the history of the Candlelight line, Dell has tried to maintain a high standard of excellence, to give you the finest in reading pleasure. It is now and will remain our most ardent ambition.

Vivian Stephens
Editor
Candlelight Romances

Chapter One

Sometimes it seemed as if the mist that clouded her memory was about to lift. Any number of things might trigger this suspenseful feeling. A certain slant of light, snatches of music overheard on another patient's radio, the sound of laughter—even the smell of newsprint or of rain-dampened wool or the scent of roses had caused it. It lasted for only a matter of seconds before, as quickly as it had begun, it was gone. Then the mist descended again, as impenetrable as ever.

Dr. Ziegler had counseled her simply to relax when it occurred. He said this would make it easier for her memories to surface, but so far this had proved to be impossible advice to follow. Inevitably, when the feeling waned, she was tense with the prospect of self-discovery; her forehead was dewed by perspiration, and she was weak and shaking from the strain of trying to remember.

By the beginning of her third week at the hospital, she had recovered enough from her injuries so that she was fully ambulatory. As her physical condition improved, her restlessness increased, leading her to spend a part of each day visiting the children in the pediatric ward. She read them stories or played games with them, and the overworked nurses were grateful to have the services of a volunteer who was willing to help entertain the youngsters.

It was among the toys in their playroom that she found the cowrie shell. She touched it with wondering fingers, thinking that it was a peculiar artifact to find in such a place; for Green River, Wyoming, was hundreds of miles inland and half a world away from tropical seas. When, in her turn, she held it to her ear, she heard the roar of the ocean that was forever trapped within the pearly prison of the shell, and this sound caused the past to glimmer more brightly than ever before through the dark veil of amnesia.

That night, for the first time since her admission to the hospital, her sleep was broken by a dream. At first it was lovely. She was racing along a beach beside an endless sea. The shore was dotted with bathers, the sand was fine and white, and the sky was a vast and cloudless blue, its purity marred only by the faint white ribbon of a single vapor-trail far, far above. She was running so fast, she seemed to be flying, and her feet seemed hardly to touch the ground as she dodged the lacy foam of the surf. As she ran she was laughing, though the sound of her joy was muted by the crash of the breakers. Now and again she glanced back over her shoulder but she knew that her reluctance to be overtaken by whoever was following her was only a pretense and that she really wanted to be caught.

Nevertheless she ran on and on, leaving the more crowded beach behind and finally rounding a rocky headland to duck behind an outcropping of boulders. In this secluded spot she paused, leaning against the roughness of the sun-drenched stone to catch her breath as the spray from the waves breaking on the rock washed over her. She sensed the approach of the man who pursued her, and her heart thumped wildly with expectation.

Suddenly the scene shifted. She was in a sort of roofless cave that was formed by the narrow cleft between two boulders and she was submerged in the warmth of her lover's arms, drowning in the excitement of his kiss. She was borne gently downward until she lay with him in the cool shadow of the rocks; so vivid was her dream that she could feel the grainy texture of the sand beneath her back. She felt the sand accommodating itself to the curve of her spine as he covered her body with the urgent weight of his.

She rejoiced in his closeness, in the strength and heat and hardness of his body, in the silky friction of his skin rubbing against hers as their limbs entwined. She threw her head back and opened her eyes to see a lone gull soaring overhead, its white wings arcing against the pristine blue backdrop of the sky, the sole witness to their loving.

But when she tried to look at her lover's face, she awoke. The dream was gone and he was gone, and she was terribly, frighteningly alone. Still trembling with the remnant of her passionate response to the anonymous man of her dream, she stared into the darkness of her room.

It had seemed so real. *He* had seemed so real—more real than the people she saw daily at the hospital. Was it possible he was someone from out of her past, or was he merely a phantom invented by her subconscious? Had she actually lived the events in the dream, or were they sheer fantasy?

Against her better judgment, because the dream had assumed such importance to her, she put these questions to Dr. Ziegler when she saw him later that day. He studied her, furrowing his brow and stroking his beard contemplatively for a few moments before he answered, giving her a typically ambiguous reply.

"It's possible your dream has some basis in fact," he told her, and she felt a bubble of elation rise within her. Then he continued smugly, "Of course it's much more likely that your dream was pure sexual indulgence."

The bubble burst, but she allowed none of her disappointment to show. She suspected that Dr. Ziegler derived some kind of perverted pleasure from encouraging her to hope, only to shatter that hope once again. During her stay at the hospital she had learned that he was a self-styled proponent of Freudian theories and from her own sessions with him she knew he tended to ascribe sexual motives to any and every type of behavior, not because of any profound scientific persuasion but because he had a remarkably smutty mind.

With his carefully cultivated Vandyke and close-cropped hair, he even tried to resemble Freud. But for all this emulation of his idol, she thought he looked like nothing more than a distinctly unsavory cartoon character plucked straight from the pages of *MAD* magazine.

"At any rate," he added grudgingly, "the mystery of your identity may soon be solved, despite your lack of cooperation with me. The police believe they have located your relatives."

Though she pleaded with him to give her more

details about this exhilarating possibility, he refused to do so.

Even with this rather cryptic warning, she experienced not the slightest flicker of recognition when she first saw Garth Falconer. He and Dr. Ziegler were on the far side of the solarium talking with Miss McKenna, the day nurse. Miss McKenna's cool blond prettiness was enlivened by uncharacteristic animation as she sparkled up at him, and her only reactions were curiosity and mild amusement over the nurse's openly flirtatious manner with the stranger.

He was perhaps a little less than six feet in height, but he was so slender that he appeared to be much taller than this. From the width of his shoulders beneath the expensive cut of the sport jacket he was wearing, she decided his leanness was deceptive and that he was probably quite muscular in a lithe, wiry way—like a dancer or a marathon runner. Even from a distance she could sense the raw vitality he exuded. It set him apart and made him seem glaringly out of place in the environment of the hospital.

His thick, springy hair was the rich color of mahogany and though she could not see what color they were, his eyes were large and wide-spaced beneath well-marked brows. There was an austerity about his cleanly chiseled features, and a self-confidence bordering on arrogance that stamped his patrician good looks with an air of unrelenting pride and authority. If he'd lived a few centuries ago, he might have been a crusader—or a conquistador. She could envision his eyes, whatever their color, burning with passionate conviction and she could easily imagine him choosing death before dishonor.

For some reason this idea caused her a vague uneasiness, but she shrugged it off, telling herself that the man was only a stranger after all, and his personal brand of ethics was no concern of hers. The warning ignored, she returned her straying attention to the elderly woman seated nearby.

"Now don't that beat all!" Mrs. Jenkins remarked as she, too, gazed in the direction of the nurse and the men with her. "Who'd have thought that young woman could ever so much as crack a smile? She can't be bothered to look halfway pleasant for the sake of the patients around here." She shook her head and pursed her lips thoughtfully. "It's such a shame," she lamented. "Miss McKenna is real pretty when she doesn't look like she just swallowed a mouthful of vinegar."

Mrs. Jenkins beckoned her to move closer and lowered her voice to a whisper. "You know who the younger man with her is, don't you? It's Garth Falconer. He used to be something of a celebrity on the racing circuit. I recollect reading that his father died, and he left auto racing to take over the family business. As I recall, it had to do with heavy construction."

"Tsk, tsk! Gossiping *again*, Mrs. Jenkins?" Her doctor, a portly, well-barbered man who had just joined them, scolded her mockingly. Though he was wagging his head reproachfully, he smiled at the object of his teasing as she patted her blue-rinsed hair, assuring herself her marcelled waves were tucked into her hairnet. The lively octogenarian was recovering from surgery to repair a broken hip. She was something of a pet with the hospital staff and Dr. Forsythe was not immune to her appeal.

"Don't get on your high horse with me, Doc!" Mrs. Jenkins's currant-dark eyes twinkled coquettishly. "I was just thinking that for all their carrying on, youngsters nowadays don't know beans about enjoying themselves. If you ask me, things are backward to what they ought to be. Folks should start out as senior citizens and get younger every year. As it is, by the time a body learns how to have a good time, they're too old to put what they've learned into practice!"

"Ah, Mrs. Jenkins," Dr. Forsythe responded with a show of regretful gallantry, "if only I were twenty years older, I'd be very tempted to show you how wrong you are."

"Hogwash! If you were twenty years older, you young whippersnapper, you'd be too old for me!"

The doctor laughed heartily. "Since you prefaced your comment by calling me 'young,' I'll forgive you for the rest of that sentiment, Mrs. J." He surveyed her silently for a moment and nodded his approval. "I can tell by your sharp tongue and sharper wit that you're feeling much improved today. As a matter of fact, I think it's safe to predict you'll be ready to go home soon, but for the time being, how about coming back to your room so I can check you over?"

His manner was courtly as he helped his patient to her feet and offered his arm for her to lean on.

"See you later, kiddo," Mrs. Jenkins called back as the doctor escorted her from the room. "Keep your fingers crossed that I'll pass the physical so my grandson can spring me from this god-awful place tomorrow. As I always say, a hospital is no place for sick people!"

Smiling at the appearance the two of them presented—Dr. Forsythe so nattily dressed and stockily built, Mrs. Jenkins shrunken and birdlike, wearing a rumpsprung housecoat of faded blue chenille—she watched their slow departure from the solarium. Her preoccupation with this prevented her from detecting Garth Falconer's approach until he stood directly in front of her.

"Hello, Julie," he said softly.

She looked up at him slowly. If he'd been impressive seen from a distance, at this range his virile good looks were intimidating. Now that he was close, she could see that his eyes were a changeable gray-green with tawny flecks of gold that might sometimes warm their cool depths.

"I'm sorry," she apologized stiltedly after a tense silence had spun out between them. "Do I know you?"

"So it's true," he said grimly, apparently having decided she honestly had no recollection of ever having met him. "You really do have amnesia."

"I'm sorry," she repeated gently. "Do we know each other well?"

"Before you took off without bothering to say 'so long,' there was a time when I *thought* we did." He laughed and the quality of his laughter was ironical and mirthless. "You're my wife."

Her eyes widened incredulously as she studied his face, searching for a clue that this was some sort of practical joke, but his expression was totally serious. The only emotion he displayed was anger when a muscle leaped along the angle of his jaw.

She glanced swiftly down at her hands. They were fine-boned and narrow, with slender graceful fingers that at the moment were nervously clutching the

14

rough folds of her hospital robe. She was wearing no rings; no jewelry of any kind.

The upholstery of the sofa gave beneath his weight as he sat beside her and she raised her eyes to see that he was holding one hand extended toward her. A broad wedding band with an antique filigree design lay in the palm of his hand.

"Take it," he directed harshly. "It's yours."

The ring seemed to swim before her eyes and all at once she felt disoriented and dizzy. The room tilted crazily about her and when she closed her eyes to try to stem the attack of vertigo, it increased in severity until she swayed weakly and her sense of equilibrium deserted her completely.

His hands were strong and sure as they forced her head down into the hard yet strangely comforting hollow of his shoulder. He held her there while the room gradually righted itself and the earth settled on its axis once again.

"There must be some mistake," she protested in a small voice that was further muffled by the nubby fabric of his jacket. "I *couldn't* have forgotten such an important thing as being married."

"There's no mistake," he said evenly. "The authorities have been extremely careful to make a positive identification."

"But how—"

"They've checked your fingerprints against those on your driver's license."

"So it's true," she whispered.

A soft sigh escaped her as she moved away from him. He made no attempt to hold her against her will but allowed her to put some distance between them. She glanced up at him but found she was not prepared to confront the battery of his eyes and hurriedly averted her face. Concentrating on her hands, which were now clasped tightly in her lap, she sought to regain a semblance of composure.

"Your name is Julie Falconer," he said. "Your maiden name was Hastings. And I'm Garth Falconer."

"I know," she acknowledged flatly. "One of the patients recognized you and pointed you out to me."

She felt acutely self-conscious and raising one shaky hand, she pressed it to her temple to form a facsimile of a blinder to conceal herself from his view.

"Do you remember anything?" asked Garth.

She laughed and was startled by the bitter tone of it. "I remember many things—all of them impersonal. It's people and places I can't recall. I didn't even know my own name. They've been calling me Jane Smith here at the hospital."

"Do you remember the accident?"

The bluntness of the question took her breath away. She was stunned, and her eyes were shadowed and haunted when she turned toward him.

"Oh, yes," she replied brokenly. "I only wish I didn't."

Even speaking of it in passing, she relived the horror. One moment the bus had been moving powerfully up the steep stretch of highway toward the mountain pass, and the next a huge boulder had plummeted down on it from above. At first it had appeared relatively harmless, bouncing across the macadam surface as lightly as if it were only a stage prop. There had been the squeal of brakes and a few screams as the bus gave a sickening lurch. Its wheels

16

slipped and spun, striving to find a safe purchase on the shoulder of the roadway. Then had come the awful grinding of metal as it lost the battle with gravity and rolled. The passengers were white-faced, their mouths stretched wide in silent terror.

She'd been thrown clear when the emergency exit by her seat gave way and a stunted pine tree near th· top of the ravine had broken her fall. Helplessly she had watched while the bus rolled again and again, like some gigantic beast in its death throes, until finally it was suspended in space, disappearing over the brink of the precipice to fall smoothly away into nothingness.

When she heard the final agonizing crash—mindless of pain, stumbling and sliding, sometimes clawing for handholds—she worked her way down to the edge of the cliff. She had seen the bright flames blossom until they enveloped the silver metal and when at last the fire had consumed itself, there was no sign of life about the charred, twisted hulk that was all that remained of the bus.

For a long time she'd stared down at the wreckage, praying that there were other survivors, praying for the impossible. Unable to encompass the loss of over thirty lives, her grief had centered on the girl who'd been seated across the aisle from her. She'd overheard enough of her conversation to know she was on her way to Laramie to enroll in classes at the University of Wyoming. How old was she? Julie had wondered. Seventeen, perhaps. Eighteen at the most.

Julie wished she'd been more receptive to the girl's overtures toward conversation. She wished she'd known the girl's name. Her face, beautiful in its youthful intensity, glowing with hope and promise, had floated before Julie's eyes, and it was more than she could bear: to think of that hope going unrewarded, the promise denied, the girl dying before she'd ever had a chance to live.

Anguishing because she was alive when so many were dead, she had questioned why she should have been the one to survive.

"Why?" she whispered. She'd turned away from the still-smoking ruin at the bottom of the gorge to look up at the implacable heights that had spawned the boulder. Near hysteria, she screamed, *"Why?"*

A starburst of pain had exploded inside her head and, for a time, there had been blessed oblivion.

"Are you all right?" Garth Falconer asked, calling her back to the present.

She stared at him as if she were seeing him for the first time. His brows were drawn and the bones of his face seemed more prominent, as if they were carved from granite. It was some time before she realized he'd taken her hand in order to slip the ring on her finger. She was still holding his hand, gripping it so tightly that her fingers felt numb and bloodless.

Still shivering slightly from the awful images he'd revived, she nodded and made a conscious effort to relax her grip on him. The ring fit perfectly, but its dull gold luster looked out of place against her pale skin, and it was so heavy, it seemed to weigh her down. She jammed her left hand into the pocket of the robe and still she was painfully aware of the ring.

As if he'd read her mind, Garth explained, "We haven't been married very long."

"Did we have some kind of disagreement?"

"No," he replied tersely.

Her eyes were clouded with perplexity when they met his. "Then why did I leave?"

"I'm not sure." His expression was shuttered, giving her not the least indication of his emotions.

"And it took you until now to find me?"

He nodded. "Nearly four weeks," he said tonelessly.

And did you care at all? she wondered. Aloud she asked, "Have I other relatives?"

"Only an uncle, Rupert Hastings, and his wife and daughter. Your parents died when you were a child and after that you lived with your maternal grandmother. She died a little over a year ago."

Julie was silent as she assimilated this information. After a time Garth observed in a dry voice, "I gather none of these vital statistics spark any memories."

"No," she said dully. "I'm sorry, but they don't."

He glanced about them as though calculating whether the few patients remaining in the solarium at this twilight hour could overhear their conversation.

"I should have thought of it sooner," she reluctantly offered, "but perhaps you'd like to continue this in my room. We'd have more privacy there."

"This is fine," he replied curtly. "We'll have all the privacy we need tomorrow. Your doctors tell me you're well enough to be discharged, and I'll be taking you home."

Panic dried her mouth and constricted her throat, making speech impossible. It must have shown in her eyes as well because, for the first time since the beginning of their interview, Garth's expression softened.

"There's nothing to be afraid of, Julie," he reassured her. "I won't make any demands you're not prepared to meet."

He touched her face; his palm was warm and hard against the softness of her cheek. It was a soothing, almost avuncular gesture. The last rays of the dying sun burnished his hair and seemed to settle in the tawny flecks in his eyes, and she wondered how she could ever have thought them cold. And when he smiled, his spare features were transformed; they had about them an almost boyish good humor. His face was made for smiling, she thought. She found herself charmed into believing his promise.

"Where is home?" she asked.

"In northern California in an area that's known as the Valley of the Moon," he replied. His smile broadened at her startled expression. "It's in the wine country north of San Francisco, not far from Santa Rosa," he explained. "The nearest town is Sonoma."

He studied her face closely as he told her this, and it was clear that she was discouraged.

"It doesn't ring any bells, does it," he said and his unexpected gentleness brought a hot rush of tears to her eyes.

"No," she replied tremulously, "except that I don't think I'm terribly familiar with the general area you've described."

"Well, that's not surprising. You lived there until you were about five, but you returned for the first time only a few months ago. It will all come back to you eventually."

"Dr. Ziegler believes I might be helped by hypnosis."

Garth nodded. "He mentioned it to me too. He

also said he'd tried to hypnotize you and found you were resistant to it."

"I'm resistant to *him*!" She wrinkled her nose with distaste. "I don't like him."

Amused by her vehemence, Garth chuckled. "Now I understand why he took his failure as a personal insult! We'll just have to find a therapist you do trust, won't we."

Chapter Two

The sight of herself in a mirror was still something of a shock to Julie. Even after four weeks it was like seeing a stranger. Of course for the first couple of weeks her features had been so battered and swollen, she had looked like the loser of a barroom brawl. The doctors kept telling her how lucky she was that her facial wounds were superficial, for she might have been badly scarred. But even when the swelling had subsided, she mostly tried to avoid looking at herself at all, and when it became absolutely necessary, she concentrated on one feature at a time or on the action of combing her hair or washing her face.

The following morning, however, she studied herself carefully, critical of the hospital pallor of the face that confronted her. It was a small oval of a face that was framed by a silky spill of dark hair. She supposed her eyes were her best feature—or they would be, if they weren't so lackluster. From beneath fine level brows they stared back at her, so velvety and dark a brown that they were almost as black as her hair. They tilted upward slightly at the corners, which gave them a certain piquancy, and they were surrounded by an abundance of long sooty lashes, but they were far too large for the rest of her face—so large, they practically swallowed the rest of her. Their expression was dazed. She thought she looked as if she were sleepwalking even though she was wide-awake.

She turned impatiently away from her reflection. Taken separately, all of her features were disproportionate. Not only were her eyes too big but her mouth was too full, her nose was too short, and her neck too long. Her chin had a funny little cleft that was slightly off-center. It looked as if it had been added as an afterthought and it made her appear fey and impish.

She saw nothing in her image that a man like Garth Falconer might find appealing. He was such a magnificent creature, it was only logical that he should have a comparable paragon for a wife. He deserved a woman who never had to worry about dandruff or split ends, who never scratched or perspired—at least in public. His wife shouldn't succumb to nail-biting and if she cried, she should do even that beautifully.

But then, she knew very little about Garth while he knew a disturbing amount about her. She felt uneasily at a disadvantage with him because of this.

Yet for all his physical perfection Garth claimed he didn't know why she'd run away. What was it he'd said when she'd asked about this? His reply had been evasive, something about not being sure. He'd glossed over the subject so quickly that she hadn't really noticed it at the time. But certainly his answer implied that he had a good idea what had prompted her to take flight and, for reasons of his own, didn't want to reveal it to her.

Julie thought that on the surface their reunion had

been a strangely emotionless one, especially since they were newlyweds. When he'd left for his motel the night before, he'd drawn her to him with one arm negligently about her shoulders and kissed her lightly on the forehead. For an instant, she'd had an impulse to put her own arms around him and lift her mouth for his kiss. She had wanted to do this so badly, it had taken all the strength of her will not to.

Instead, she'd met his eyes directly and with an elaborate display of casualness, she'd said, "Good night."

His arm had tightened about her, his fingers digging threateningly into the soft flesh of her upper arm, and amusement kindled the golden sparks in the depths of his eyes, turning them a fiery green.

"My name is Garth," he reminded her silkily. "Use it."

"G-good night, *G-Garth.*"

"Again," he commanded. "And this time, try to say it like you mean it."

"Good night, Garth," she complied throatily, making his name sound like an endearment.

"Good night, Julie," he said softly.

For a moment she'd thought he might kiss her once more, but he'd only touched a fingertip to the dimple in her chin, turned on his heel, and walked away from her. He'd pushed through the swinging door of the hospital entrance and disappeared into the darkness, leaving her with an empty feeling of dissatisfaction.

Sighing, Julie turned back to the mirror. She refused to engage in further speculation about Garth Falconer and fixed her attention on arranging the jabot at the neckline of her blouse. He was due to arrive in a few minutes, and intuition told her that he disliked being kept waiting.

"Yoo-hoo, kiddo." A rapid series of knocks that was a private signal between them preceded Mrs. Jenkins as she opened the door wide enough to pop her head in. With her blue-white hair unconfined by its customary net and her head cocked to one side, she looked more than ever like a jolly sparrow.

"Come in, Mrs. Jenkins," Julie invited.

"Got any coffee going begging this morning?" Mrs. Jenkins asked hopefully.

"Yes, I have. If you'd like to sit down, I'll get some for you."

"Don't mind if I do."

Mrs. Jenkins limped to the chair nearest the door while Julie went to the breakfast tray by her bed to fetch the cup. This had become a daily routine, and she no longer needed to ask how her visitor took her coffee.

"I don't know why the coffee on my tray is always stone-cold," Mrs. Jenkins complained mildly. "Yours is always nice and hot and they serve us from the same cart."

"And I don't even like coffee," Julie said as she handed the elderly lady her cup. "I much prefer tea, but even though I request it when I mark my menu for the day, they never bring it."

Mrs. Jenkins sampled the steaming beverage and leaned back in her chair. "Aaah!" she exclaimed blissfully, "you've put in just the right amount of sugar today. I don't know what I'll do for my morning coffee now that you're leaving. Doctor Forsythe says he'd like to keep me here a few more days."

Her button-bright eyes gleamed above the rim of

her cup as she looked Julie up and down. "Fancy you being married to Garth Falconer. I've never met anyone so closely related to a real live celebrity before. I saw Evel Knievel once. It was before his Snake River Canyon jump. But that was only from a distance and I never got to *meet* him."

"If you'd like to meet Garth, I'll introduce you," Julie offered. She knew it was what Mrs. Jenkins expected. "He should be here soon."

"Would you, dear? That's mighty sweet of you." Mrs. Jenkins beamed at her. "My grandson will be so impressed when he hears about this. He was a big fan of your husband's when he was racing."

"I'm sure it will be Garth's pleasure, Mrs. Jenkins."

"What will be my pleasure?" called Garth as he strode into the room. He seemed to bring the invigorating freshness of the outdoors in with him, and the atmosphere was subtly charged with his vitality.

"This is Mrs. Jenkins, Garth," Julie said. "She's been looking forward to meeting you."

Garth held Mrs. Jenkins's hand between both of his and bowed slightly from the waist, smiling down at her.

"It is indeed my pleasure, ma'am," he said. He solemnly kissed her hand before he released it.

"Oh, my! Aren't you the one!" Mrs. Jenkins fanned the air with the hand he'd kissed. "I'm all aflutter. I may never wash this hand again."

Laughing, Garth turned toward Julie. This morning, m~king the most of Mrs. Jenkins's presence, he fol r in his arms and whispered close to her ear, ldn't want to disappoint your romantic d you?"

She was tense within the circle of his arms as he touched his mouth to hers, but he prolonged the soft contact of his lips only until he'd won her rather tentative response to the heady sensation of his kiss. And again she was left dissatisfied when he freed her.

"We'd better get moving, Julie," he announced briskly. "I've already squared accounts with the business office, and your doctor has signed your release, so if you'd care to finish getting your things together, we can be on our way."

She crossed to the bedside stand to retrieve the small brown paper bag that contained all of her known belongings. In it were a comb and hairbrush, a toothbrush, and a few toilet articles the hospital had provided. It struck her as a pathetic amount for a young woman of twenty-three or so to be able to call her own.

Attempting jauntiness, she said, "This is it," as she folded the top of the sack to close it.

Garth's eyes narrowed as they traveled over her, taking in the disreputable state of her skirt and blouse. Both garments had been bloodstained and badly torn in the accident. Some of the mends were clearly visible, while most of the stains hadn't been removed entirely by the laundry. If one could go by the seam bindings, the skirt had once been a lovely rose-pink, but now it was a nondescript grayish taupe. The jacket that had completed the ensemble had been beyond repair, and she had lost her shoes as well. One of the nurses had given her a pair of down-at-the-heel sandals to wear for the trip home, but they were too large, and she had to walk with a stiff-footed gait in order to keep them on her feet.

Suddenly she realized how terribly out of place she

looked compared to Garth, and for the first time she was embarrassed by her tattered clothing. Her cheeks flamed with the rush of color that flooded them, and she resented being made so aware of the contrast between them by his appraisal of her.

His eyes were cold this morning: a gray that was unrelieved by any trace of gold or green in spite of the dusky gold of his cotton knit shirt.

"Could I trouble you to walk me back to my room before you leave, Mr. Falconer?" Mrs. Jenkins asked, flirting with him quite shamelessly.

"Certainly," he agreed equably, "but only on the condition that you call me Garth."

"And you must call me Lydia," she gushed as he helped her out of the chair. "I do appreciate this, Garth. It's hard for me to get about on my own, you see. But I won't take too much of your time. My room is almost next door."

Actually Lydia Jenkins's room was at the opposite end of the corridor, but no one was likely to quibble with her over her shading of the truth.

"Good-bye, Mrs. Jenkins," Julie called after her visitor as, shortening his stride to allow for her snail's pace, Garth guided her into the hall.

"Don't do anything I wouldn't do, kiddo," Mrs. Jenkins advised, favoring Julie with her puckish smile. "But if you can't help yourself, remember what I always say: Anything worth doing is worth doing *twice* !"

By the time she was seated in the car Garth had rented, Julie had fanned her resentment into a simmering pitch of anger that destroyed the delight she would otherwise have taken in the blue and gold splendor of Wyoming's Indian summer. As it was, she derived no pleasure at all from the warmth of the sun that angled in through the open window to caress her cheek and forearm.

Her "thank you" to Garth when he handed her into the sedan was frostily formal, and he slanted a knowing look at her as he climbed behind the wheel. He made no move to start the engine. After jingling the keys a few times in his palm, he sat perfectly still for so long a time that she began to feel foolish in her disapproving pose. She stirred uneasily in the luxuriously upholstered bucket seat.

"All right," Garth said. "Out with it."

She glanced at him covertly and saw that a smile was tugging at the corners of his mouth. Stung by his amusement, she bit back a furious torrent of speech and maintained her stony silence. When he spoke again, his tone was amiable and unconcerned.

"Perhaps I should inform you that I can outstubborn you any day of the week."

"And I suppose you think that's something to be proud of!" she said, lashing out hotly.

"Damned right, I do," ne agreed blandly. "So you might as well tell me what's bothering you, because we're not going anywhere till you do—not if we have to stay here all day."

"Very well," she said stiffly. "You promised you wouldn't make any demands on me and already you've gone back on your word."

"Correction! I said I wouldn't make any demands you're not prepared to meet."

"But you *kissed* me this morning!" She glared at him accusingly.

"So?" He shrugged. "Can you honestly say you

29

didn't enjoy it?" His eyes refused to relinquish their hold on hers. However badly she might want to look away, she watched, mesmerized, as they darkened and settled on her soft pink mouth. When she made no reply, he leaned closer and murmured, "I think what's really eating you is that I haven't been demanding *enough* !"

This time Garth's kiss quickly progressed from tenderly insistent to frankly sensuous, and her response was immediate, intense, and undeniable. She matched his passion with an unexpected voluptuousness of her own. Her lips moved eagerly beneath his, her breathing quickened, her heartbeat raced until it mingled so thoroughly with his that she could not have said where hers ended and his began. But when her lips parted enticingly, wanting him to deepen the kiss, he declined the invitation. She sensed that he was deliberately withholding this further intimacy from her, and his rigid control was frustrating, maddening.

It dawned on her that he was doing this to prove his claim that she wanted him to be more demanding, and it was she who moved away.

Julie was shaken by what she'd learned about herself. Until that kiss, if she'd been asked to characterize in a single word her manner toward the opposite sex, the word she would have chosen was *reserved*. While admittedly this was not from any specific knowledge she had about the kind of woman she was, she instinctively felt the appropriateness of it. Now she knew that her reaction to Garth was completely without reserve.

Though the pressure of his lips had been gentle, her mouth felt bruised; she was trembling, and she could no longer tell herself that he had forced her into doing anything against her will. He had touched her only with his lips. She had been held captive solely by the sweetness of his soft exploration of her mouth.

She was dismayed at the ease with which he could arouse her. She knew that her expression was far too revealing and tried to keep her eyes downcast, but he cupped her chin with his hand and made her look at him.

"It's a relief to know you haven't forgotten how to do that." He smiled down at her engagingly. "I guess it's like riding a bicycle. Your mind may not remember, but your body does."

"Please," she pleaded raggedly. "Don't laugh at me."

"I won't," he said softly. "Not about this. Never about this."

Julie touched her mouth with one hand and quickly, almost frantically, ran her fingertips over her delicately molded brows and cheekbones as though by doing so, she might discover something in the unfamiliar contours of her features that would make her less a stranger to herself.

"I don't *know* myself!" she cried.

Garth stilled the hand that was restlessly searching her face with his fingers. He smoothed the hair back from her temples and said with quiet confidence, "Trust me, Julie. *I* know you."

Their glances locked, and for long moments words were unnecessary. She saw tenderness in his eyes; she saw integrity and determination. She saw that he was one thing in her life that was real and solid and reassuring, that he was someone secure and constant for her to hold on to while she found herself. And he saw the dawning of faith in her eyes.

"I have something to show you," he said.

Reaching in front of her, he flipped open the glove compartment and withdrew several photographs. The first one he handed her was a formal portrait of a wedding party—*her* wedding party. The bride's face was the one she saw when she looked in the mirror, yet it was different somehow. And the difference, hard to pinpoint though it was, was disconcerting. For the time being she avoided looking at the bride in order to study the other people in the picture.

One was a young woman of about Julie's age. She was quite lovely and very fair. Her blond hair had a pale shimmer that rivaled the ivory satin of the bridal gown.

"Your cousin Diane." Garth answered her unspoken question.

"She's very beautiful," Julie murmured. She was also very unhappy. Her smile was wide enough but it was strained. It didn't reach her eyes.

"These are her parents," Garth explained, pointing them out. "Your uncle, Rupert Hastings, and his wife, Charlotte."

Julie's brow was furrowed with concentration as she studied her uncle and aunt. They were probably in their late forties or early fifties, although it was possible that Charlotte was younger. She actually looked much younger than that, and if it hadn't been for her supercilious expression, she would have had a cameolike beauty.

Rupert Hastings was handsome, and gave an overall impression of self-assured urbanity. His posture was erect and vigorous and his skin was smooth and unlined, but there was something about him that didn't ring true. Was it a lack of character about his face? Surely there was a touch of vanity in the way his improbably dark hair was styled in deep waves about his forehead, in the tightly sucked-in stomach that made the most of his chest and the least of his waistline. And there was a slackness about his jaw that might denote an element of weakness.

"It's easy to see where Diane gets her good looks," she commented noncommittally. She found she was abstractedly rubbing her temple to ease her tension, and she was relieved to turn her attention to Garth's laughing countenance.

She smiled, unaware that she did so. His enjoyment was so apparent, she felt she shared whatever joke had prompted him to laugh so unrestrainedly for the photographer.

"Why do you look so irreverent?" she inquired lightly.

"Look at yourself," he replied dryly. "You don't look very solemn either."

"No," she conceded in a small voice. "I don't, do I."

Now she saw what it was that made the difference between Julie-in-the-mirror and Julie-the-bride. The bride was laughing as merrily as Garth. She was radiant with happiness, and it was happiness that gave her the lively beauty that made her worthy of such a husband.

Garth handed her another picture. This one showed the bride and groom dancing, with Garth holding Julie-the-bride as if she were as fragile as porcelain and infinitely precious to him. While they danced, they gazed at one another so longingly, it was as if they were making love to one another in their thoughts, with their eyes.

She felt like a voyeur, viewing such an intimate exchange, and hurriedly passed the wedding photographs back to him.

"No comment?" Garth raised an eyebrow at her. "This is the last one," he said as he held out the final picture.

It was a candid shot, blurred and out of focus, but in spite of the poor quality of the picture she recognized the locale. She recognized the beach, the cloudless sky, the sparkling turquoise sea, the rocky headland in the distance. She *knew* the Julie in the picture. She had felt her joy, experienced her excitement, her anticipation.

She was light-headed and she closed her eyes tightly. "Where was this taken?" she asked. Her voice was barely audible.

"Near Carmel." Garth's breath was warm on her cheek, and she knew he was watching her closely. "Do you remember it?"

"I had a dream about a place like this."

"I took that snapshot of you on our honeymoon." Garth's tone was low and urgent. "You were at your uncooperative best! You refused to stand still long enough for me to get you in the viewfinder. You kept racing the waves and playing in the surf and splashing me until I finally got fed up with your pranks and threatened to throw you in the water. Then you ran away down the beach toward the rocks with me hot on your trail, and when I caught you—"

"Don't," she protested weakly. "Please don't."

"I didn't throw you in, Julie," he finished softly.

"In my dream I couldn't see your face. Even after I woke up, I felt so lost and afraid."

"Then look at me now, Julie."

Slowly she complied. Relief washed over her when she saw the gold flecks were back in his eyes. He was so near, she could make out the nearly invisible line of his beard. Her gaze wandered hungrily over the clean line of his jaw, along the leanness of his cheeks and the proud jut of his nose to return to his eyes.

"You see!" He grinned triumphantly. "There's nothing to be afraid of now."

"But I still can't remember, except for that one thing."

"That's a beginning. We'll just have to work a bit harder on the rest."

He brushed his knuckles against the point of her jaw in a mock blow designed to offer encouragement, telling her she could roll with the punches.

"At least I've gained your confidence," he said.

Buoyed by his optimism, she smiled back at him as she nodded her agreement.

Chapter Three

All one had to do was read a road map of Wyoming and the spirit of the state became clear. Julie was fascinated by the place names on the map Garth had tossed into her lap when they'd left Green River, asking her to be navigator and chart their course to Kemmerer.

The rivers for instance. Not only were their names descriptive of their courses and character, they were poetic as well.

Here was the Powder River, which was synonymous with the Old West. There were the Sweetwater and the Bitter, the Yellowstone and the Snake. Here was the Platte, reputed to be too yellow to drink and too thin to paint with. But of them all her favorite was the Wind River. Surely it must be as powerful and persevering as its namesake. It must be a stream that was tireless enough to carve great chasms through solid stone. A stream that was changeable; by turns swift-flowing or gentle. Fickle enough to suddenly change its name and become the Big Horn.

Some of the names of the towns might reflect the attitude of their pioneer settlers toward them. Here was Dull Center and only thirty miles away was a town named Bright, perhaps in honor of the governor who was instrumental in legislating the vote for women. There were Superior and Freedom—and Goose Egg.

At the end of a back road in the middle of nowhere was a town called Halfway. Halfway to where? she wondered. To heaven? To civilization? To Oregon perhaps?

There was Hole in the Wall, a reminder of outlaw gangs and posses, of ambush and lynch law. And how could one see the words *Alkali Flat* and *not* feel the harshness of the place?

The Indian names were particularly colorful. Medicine Bow and Spotted Horse, Ten Sleep and Sundance—each of these names must be worth at least a thousand pictures.

There was Hell's Half Acre and Paradise Valley, and Julie thought that these two names illustrated the violent diversity of this land; it might well serve as a caldron in nature's laboratory, so infinite was its variety. From its snow-capped mountain ranges to the canyons and dry washes of its badlands, from the rich grasslands of its prairies to the arid sage of its deserts, it was tempered by the glaring heat of summer and by winter's arctic chill and, except for an ocean, there was at least one of everything here.

She felt an affinity for its unyielding terrain. In fact, when they'd driven away from the hospital this morning, she'd been so intrigued by it that she hadn't immediately noticed that they were traveling in a direction that took them away from the airport at Rock Springs. It was not until Garth pulled into the parking lot of a general store that she'd realized that fact.

"Why are we stopping here?" she asked.

"You'll need some clothes," Garth replied. "I'm sorry I didn't think of it sooner, or I'd have brought some of your things with me."

"Surely that's not necessary just for the flight home!"

"We're not going home for a while," he countered as he ushered her into the building. "We're going to take some time together to become reacquainted. I thought we'd head for Jackson Hole for a few days. There's someone there I'd like to see."

Her step faltered and her eyes were wide with astonishment as she looked up at him. "But, Garth—"

"Don't argue, Julie," he said firmly. "Trust me."

She had. As he had advised, she selected some jeans and shirts, several changes of underwear, a fleece-lined denim vest, and a warm bulky knit sweater. It had been a relief to exchange the ill-fitting sandals for desert boots of glove-soft suede.

She was surprised by Garth's patience as he waited for her to make her choices and try things on in the cluttered stockroom of the store.

At his suggestion she'd included a couple of less casual outfits; the cream-colored pantsuit that she was now wearing and a long dress fashioned of a fine synthetic. It felt wonderfully silky next to her skin, and its splashy print of sunset colors was flattering to her midnight-dark hair and eyes. They even found a handbag and some sandals, which were her size, that she could wear with the dress.

"Is there anything else you need?" Garth asked.

She shook her head doubtfully. "I can't think of anything."

By now she was beginning to feel a bit tired from

the emotional upheavals of the morning and the unaccustomed activity of the shopping. Her knees were suddenly too shaky to support her, and she leaned against the counter, watching without participating in the consultation that took place between Garth and the clerk regarding cosmetics and stockings and accessories.

The salesgirl was very attractive in a robust, earthy way. Though she was no more than high school age, she had an aura of sexuality that was unmistakable. With rapidly fading amusement Julie observed that her technique was as well developed as her figure. She practiced her hot-eyed glances and moist-lipped smiles on Garth, fluttering her lashes and walking with a sinuous swing of her hips that was so exaggerated, it would have been comical had it not been so skillfully done.

I'll bet her eyelashes are false, Julie wagered silently. It made her even more disgruntled than before to have to admit she had sunk to that level of bitchiness, but the girl's blatant seductiveness set her teeth on edge. Garth might not be encouraging the salesgirl's behavior, but he certainly wasn't doing anything to discourage it.

"I'm going to wait in the car," she announced shortly, stalking out of the store before he could stop her.

Though it was early October, the temperature was in the eighties; with the sun beating down, even with the windows open, the inside of the car was stifling. Julie removed her jacket and undid the topmost buttons of her blouse, but all too soon the heat became intolerable.

What was taking Garth so long? she wondered

crossly as she climbed out of the car to wander toward the belt of cottonwoods that bordered one side of the parking area. A cooling breeze fanned her flushed cheeks. After the airless interior of the sedan it was delightfully refreshing under the trees.

She found a bench in the shady grove and sat looking at the river. It made a lazy curve around this small peninsula; its waters looked serene and its muddy-green surface was darkened intermittently by the wind. She threw some pebbles in, one by one, and watched the concentric spreading of the ripples.

Downstream, on the far shore, the channel was defined by sheer bluffs that rose a hundred feet or more and flat-topped buttes that assumed a tarnished-copper hue where the sun struck them.

Under the influence of this peaceful scene her mood became more placid as well. She acknowledged that she was jealous and chastised herself for allowing such a trifling incident to bother her. By the time Garth emerged from the store, she was able to respond spontaneously to his smile and say hello to him without sounding peevish.

She saw that he'd gone so far as to buy a zippered duffel bag and have her purchases packed into it for her, and she was touched by his thoughtfulness. She also felt horribly petty.

Blinking rapidly to hold back tears, she said miserably, "You think of everything."

"I try to," he returned cheerfully. As if she needed proof that nothing was too trivial to escape his notice, he added, "You're not crying, are you?"

"Of course not. It's only that the sun was in my eyes."

Though he nodded judiciously, his knowing look told her she hadn't succeeded in misleading him.

"Thank you for the clothes and everything," she said in a chastened voice as he turned onto the highway. His careless shrug dismissed the issue of being of no consequence.

Before they left Green River, they stopped at a small café for lunch. In the booth next to theirs was a family with two small daughters, perhaps three and six years old. Both of these junior sirens were captivated by Garth, but because Julie had her back to them she didn't realize they were flirting with him until she overheard their mother scolding them for their rudeness in staring. Though it had earned them their mother's disapproval, they persisted, and as she and Garth waited for their order and ate the meal, Julie was amazed to see that the unblinking attention of the little girls had rattled Garth, where the more adult techniques of Miss McKenna, Mrs. Jenkins, and the salesgirl had failed to do so.

He drummed his fingers on the tabletop, repeatedly checked his wristwatch, and hurried her through her own lunch. She was so rushed, she burned her mouth trying to gulp down her tea and finally, as a concession to him, she left it half finished.

"What are you grinning about?" he growled as they returned to the car.

She smiled sunnily up at him. "I was just thinking that you have the same effect on females of all ages."

Though Garth failed to appreciate the humor in this, Julie smiled about it again while she nodded drowsily over the road map. Her body was deliciously relaxed, and her mind wandered somewhere in the carefree limbo between sleeping and waking.

She had thought it might make her nervous to ride in a car for the first time since the accident, but Garth was an excellent driver; very smooth, very assured. Since he'd once driven in races, she supposed that was to be expected. She would have to remember to ask him about that sometime soon.

Before they'd left the café, he'd slid a cassette into the stereo; she suspected he'd done it to discourage idle conversation. She recognized both the singer and the song. It was strange that she knew James Taylor's voice, that she even knew he was performing a song composed by Carole King, yet she had no memories about herself.

"*Damn!*" Garth suddenly exclaimed, and her head snapped upright. "I thought you were going to navigate," he muttered. "Wasn't that the interchange we should have taken for Kemmerer?"

Julie was wide-awake now and she turned to look through the rear window in time to see the directional signs for the eastbound traffic.

"I'm afraid it was," she admitted timorously.

His scowl became more pronounced. "How far is it to the next exit?"

Hurriedly she checked the map. Her spirits rose when she saw it was only a short distance. "About five miles," she replied. "And there's a service road that cuts across to Highway 30, so we don't have to go too far out of our way."

He nodded. "Go back to sleep," he said brusquely. "We'll stop in Kemmerer if we can find a place to stay for the night."

"I thought you planned to drive straight through to Jackson Hole today."

"I had intended to, but you've done enough for your first day out of the hospital."

"You needn't stop on my account," she said stiffly.

"Are you so anxious to get to Jackson Hole that you can't wait till tomorrow?"

"N-no." She was startled by his coldness. Her offense in falling asleep hardly warranted his taking that attitude with her. She shook her head uncertainly and asked, "Why should I be? *How* could I be? Is that where I was going before the accident?"

"I'm not sure."

"But *you* believe that's where I was going."

"It's a possibility."

She ignored the warning of his thinly compressed mouth and doggedly pursued the issue. "You said there's someone you want to see in Jackson Hole. Who is it?"

"Will you please just leave it alone and *go back to sleep,*" he repeated roughly.

"Not till you answer me!" she exclaimed heatedly. "If it concerns me, I have a right to know."

Garth sighed. "I suppose you have a point there," he acknowledged.

They were approaching the interchange and he pulled into the exit lane. Though his eyes were trained on the road ahead, it was obvious he was brooding over the answer he should give her. In spite of this, through years of training and habit, his hands were easy in their grip on the wheel.

It was not until they reached the stop sign at the junction of the secondary road with the highway to Kemmerer that he said, "We're going to see a man by the name of Daniel Leeds."

"Daniel Leeds?" Julie echoed woodenly. "The

name by itself means nothing to me." After a tense silence she asked, "Is he a friend of mine?"

"You might say that," Garth replied sardonically. His eyes flicked over her, gray and icy. "You might even say he's a *very* good friend." He looked first to the right, then to the left to check for oncoming traffic, and the car swayed giddily as he gunned the motor and made the left turn onto Highway 30. "You might even say," he concluded crisply, "that you're in love with Daniel Leeds."

"No," she whispered. "That's impossible." Though she'd barely breathed the denial, inside she was screaming it.

She stared at Garth, staggered by the implications of his accusation. She felt winded, as if she'd sustained a blow to the solar plexus, and the bitter taste of bile filled her mouth. Breathing deeply through slightly parted lips, she fought to suppress the sensation of nausea.

The tautness of Garth's profile, the hard thrust of his jaw, were grim reminders of his pride. A man who was so fiercely proud must have a compelling reason before he would seriously entertain the idea that his wife was in love with another man. But whatever the reason, he was mistaken. He had to be.

She could not have married Garth unless she loved him. Though she had no recollection of her life before the accident, she sensed certain things about the kind of person she was and she was convinced she could never marry one man if she were in love with another one. It couldn't be true. Oh, God, she silently prayed. Don't let it be true.

"I assume you have some evidence to support your theory." She was surprised by the calmness of her voice as she challenged him. "Would you care to enlighten me?"

"Not particularly," he replied evenly. "I think I've already said too much."

Her hands were knotted so tightly that her nails bit into the softness of her palms. "You can't make an allegation like that and then refuse to discuss it! I have a right to defend myself."

"Granted. But at the moment you've had about all you can take." He glanced quickly toward her. "You're so tired that you're shaking like a leaf and you're white as a ghost."

"That's not from tiredness! It's because I'm so blasted angry!" She was also perilously close to tears.

"When you've finished your tantrum," he offered dryly, "you'll realize how tired you are."

"Tantrum!" Her voice was shrill. She was outraged by his stubbornness. Her face crumpled; tears welled in her eyes until they spilled over to run down her pale cheeks. Sniffling as quietly as she could, she tried to wipe the tears away with the backs of her hands.

"God!" Garth groaned when he heard the muted sounds of her weeping. "I might have known you'd try tears as a last resort."

The injustice of this statement caused her to cry all the harder. Garth braked sharply, and the car skidded to a stop on the shoulder of the road. Leaving the motor idling, he reached in front of her to grab a handful of tissues from the box in the glove compartment. He held them out to her, and when she didn't immediately take them, he uttered an impatient oath beneath his breath, turned the key in the ignition, and began mopping at her face himself.

At first he was so rough, he almost scoured her skin with the tissue, but his touch slowly gentled. Sighing with resignation, he gathered her in his arms to hold her close to the hard warmth of his chest, easily overcoming her halfhearted resistance to the gesture. He patted her on the back and repeatedly ran his hands over her shoulders, murmuring sympathetically until she surrendered to the temptation to be held and comforted by him. She had no idea how much time had gone by before the force of her weeping diminished to occasional hoarse, hiccuping sobs.

"I'll never understand you, Julie," Garth said at last. His voice rumbled deep in his chest and its vibrations tickled her ear. The steady beat of his heart was incredibly soothing. His shirt was sodden beneath her cheek, and she shifted slightly and plucked ineffectually at the damp spot.

"Do I usually use tears as a weapon?" she asked huskily.

"No," he admitted. "I'm sorry. It was unfair of me to imply that you do."

"I'm sorry too. I realize I must have hurt you when I ran away—"

"Let's leave that subject for now," he cut in peremptorily. "We've both had enough emotional stress for one day."

She started to protest and, sensing another flare-up of indignation, he relented. "I have nothing concrete to go on. For all I know, you and Leeds are nothing more than friends, which is why I hesitated about mentioning him at all. *Now*"—his arms tightened about her, underscoring that this was an order and not a request—"would you just drop it."

As she nodded her agreement her hair brushed his

chin, and the slight abrasiveness of his close-shaven beard against the sensitive skin of her temple ignited a tingling sensation that spread like wildfire along her nerve endings. She was acutely aware of him. The faint, tangy fragrance of his after-shave combined with the masculine essence of his sun-browned skin to create a unique and dizzying blend that filled her senses until she felt drugged by it. It reminded her of— Of what?

She felt herself hovering on the brink of remembrance and closed her eyes. She was catapulted backward in time and she saw an image, as sharp and clear as if she were watching a motion picture that was being projected onto her eyelids.

A meadow, shining fair and golden in the sunlight at the crest of a hill. The smell of dried grass. Wild flowers—were they poppies?—kindling a brilliant blaze of orange as they bobbed to the surface when the wind rustled through the undulating waves of grass. The fresh green of some kind of vines seen in the distance. And tucked snugly into the valley below, the ocher of tile roofs. A silvery garland of water that wound like tinsel through the amber folds of the hills. Red wine mellowed by the sun. A man's shadow moving with heart-stopping slowness until it blocked out the sky. . . .

As abruptly as it had begun, the vision ended. She became aware that Garth was calling her name, that his hands were locking her shoulders in a steely grip as he shook her slightly to rouse her.

"What is it, Julie?" His voice seemed to come to her from a great distance. "Are you all right?"

Her eyelids fluttered open, and she saw that he was pale under his surface layer of tan. Her pulse was racing, and she was gasping for breath as if she'd been running for miles. Her hands were clammy and her face was bathed with cold perspiration. She clutched at his forearms and was heartened by the feel of their sinewy hardness beneath her fingertips.

"What happened? God! You just seemed to go into a trance."

"It's nothing really. It's only that sometimes I can almost remember. It comes and goes without any warning."

He nodded, relieved. The color was returning to his face, and he relaxed his hold on her to move away and slump against the steering wheel, wearily running his hands through his hair. She thought that he looked every bit as tired and rumpled as she must.

"Doctor Ziegler told me about that," he said.

"I'm sorry if you were alarmed," she apologized gently. "There's no need to be."

"Did you recall anything at all?"

She was drained of energy and she leaned her head against the back of the seat, closing her eyes to make it easier to reconstruct what she'd seen as she described it.

"That sounds very much like the winery near Russian River, where you worked before we were married," Garth said when she had finished. His expression was watchful, measuring her response as he revealed, "We used to meet at the top of the hill for lunch."

"Then it's possible my memory is actually returning!"

"Your description was remarkably accurate, except for one detail. The hill where we met was much steeper than the one you saw. In fact"—he smiled in reminiscence—"the trail that leads to the top of it is so rugged, the people who live in the area call it Fat Man's Misery."

Although she couldn't stop herself from laughing along with him, she exclaimed, "That's a terrible name to give such a lovely place!"

"You had the same reaction the first time I told you that," he commented after he'd started the engine and they were traveling westward along the blacktop. "And it is a beautiful spot." His voice was softly suggestive as he added, "Romantic too."

Garth chuckled and his eyes danced roguishly, for as if on cue, Julie blushed until her entire face had turned a flattering shade of pink.

Chapter Four

Julie didn't complain when Garth told her they'd be sharing the same motel unit. Since it was Saturday, she knew they were lucky to have found a motel in Kemmerer with *any* vacancies. At least their room had two beds.

What was disturbing was the realization that she had no nightwear. Even more disconcerting was that Garth read this thought the very instant it popped into her head.

"If you'll look in your suitcase, you'll find a couple of pairs of men's pajamas." His voice was tinged with amusement as he offered this information. "You can wear the tops," he directed, "and as a special favor to you, I'll wear the bottoms."

She sat on the edge of the bed, concentrating on the toes of her shoes and turning ten shades of red.

"What's troubling you now, Julie?" Garth asked dryly. "Aren't you reassured by the fact that I've made provisions that will help you preserve your modesty? I'm not likely to ravish you after going to such lengths to do that, am I?"

Actually she had been deep in speculation about what, if anything, he normally wore in bed, but she couldn't very well ask *him* this and she hastily equivocated, "I was just wondering if I've always been so poorly organized."

"Not to my knowledge."

He continued studying her, and she glanced up at him from beneath her lashes.

"What else is on your mind?" he asked.

"Only that I do appreciate your sacrifice in wearing the bottoms," she answered tartly, nettled by his patronizing attitude. "I suppose such a show of selflessness should entitle you to tease me a bit."

Garth was not at all perturbed by her sarcasm. He only grinned his wide, boyish grin and said, "I'm glad you're big enough to make some concessions."

"Are you sure you don't want me to salaam as well?"

"A simple curtsy will do." His response was issued imperiously. "I know you'll find it as regrettable as I do, but salaaming is no longer de rigueur."

Confronted with such unabashed male arrogance, Julie was at a loss for words, and she could only stare at him, open-mouthed with amazement.

But when he turned his back on her, she tried to take advantage of the opportunity this afforded her and impulsively snatching up one of the pillows from the bed, she threw it at him. His reflexes were lightning-quick, however, and he swiveled from the hips and caught it before it came anywhere near hitting him. He crushed the pillow between his broad palms and looked menacingly down at her while she eyed him warily. He defeated her in this staring duel as well, for it was she who was the first to look away.

"You *are* getting vicious," he observed blandly. "I suppose I'd better take you out and feed you."

Now that it was dark, the air was pleasantly cool

and as they strolled the short distance to the restaurant Julie found that her irritation had already evaporated. As she walked quietly at Garth's side she asked wistfully, "Have we always fought like this?"

"Of course not, Julie," he said with suspicious solemnity. "We usually fight much more."

It never occurred to her that she might have lived in the Jackson Hole area until they were lingering over their after-dinner drinks. When she asked Garth about it, he nodded.

"Yes," he said. "Your grandparents owned a cattle ranch somewhere between the towns of Jackson and Alpine. Your grandfather died long before you were born, but your grandmother—her name was Elizabeth Ayers, by the way—tried to keep the ranch going. She had to borrow heavily, but she managed to hang on to most of the acreage until she had her first stroke. That was when you were thirteen or so.

"I gathered that over the next six or seven years her condition deteriorated to the point that she was finally forced to sell out to a neighboring rancher. The deal she made granted her a life estate in the ranch house, and you continued living there with her until she died. She'd told you she was only leasing the land to the neighbor, and it came as quite a shock when you learned otherwise."

Julie had listened intently, and when Garth concluded, she asked, "How did I happen to return to California?"

"From what you told me, while you were settling your grandmother's affairs, you found the deed to some property in Sonoma that your mother and father had owned along with receipts that indicated your grandmother had kept up the taxes on it. Before then, you'd had no idea exactly where in northern California your parents had lived and, on the spur of the moment, you decided to have a look at it."

"I wonder why my grandmother didn't tell me the truth about the ranch and my parents' property," she remarked pensively.

"You said she'd always been closemouthed about your father," Garth replied, "and evidently, as her illness progressed, her personality changed, and she became even more secretive and suspicious. She had a number of strokes, and I got the impression that in addition to that, she may have been senile. She was well into her seventies."

Introspectively she murmured, "Altogether I must have lived with her about seventeen years."

"Yes, about that long."

"That explains it then."

"Explains what?" Garth quickly probed. "Does the countryside seem familiar to you?"

"In a way," she answered vaguely, searching for words that would express her reaction to the region. "It's not that I recognize anything. It's more a feeling I have of—well, of coming home, I guess."

Both of them were lost in their own thoughts after that and they exchanged no further conversation until Garth had signaled for the check. While they stood at the cash register waiting for the hostess to bring Garth's change, he handed her their motel key.

"You could stand to have an early night," he said. "Why don't you go on ahead and turn in."

She looked up at him, puzzled. "Aren't you coming?"

"I want to make a few telephone calls first," he explained. "I'll be along soon."

Partly because she was so sleepy and partly because she recognized that this turn of events would help allay her discomfort over sharing the room with Garth, Julie didn't ask him why he'd elected to use the pay phone in the lobby when it would have been more convenient for him to make his calls from the telephone in their room.

After nearly a month of rushed morning showers, the leisureliness of a bath before retiring was heavenly and Julie stayed in the tub until she was yawning and more than ready for bed.

Unfortunately, while she was brushing her hair dry, she looked at herself in the mirror, and what she saw shocked her awake. There were still hollows beneath her cheekbones and mauve shadows under her eyes, but there was more spirit—more sparkle—in her face than she could recall having seen there before.

Was this rebirth solely a result of being away from the hospital, or was it due to Garth's company? Though she pretended to contemplate this, she realized she was kidding herself. She knew the answer very well, and she found it unnerving that in one short day Garth should have had such an impact on her.

She'd never looked at herself in a full-length mirror before and she felt uncomfortable as she did so now. Perhaps if she started from the floor and worked her way up, it would seem less vain. She tried to judge her figure objectively and concluded it wasn't half bad. A little on the thin side maybe, but one might even say it was quite nice.

She saw that she had small, high-arched feet, finely turned ankles, and long shapely legs that flared softly at the hips. From what she could make out through the folds of the towel, her waist appeared to be hand-span-narrow. And her breasts seemed to be nicely rounded—again based on what the thickness of the towel permitted her to see.

In fact, she amended, as she dared to view herself all at once from the neck down, her figure could be considered damned good!

She badly wanted to know if the reality of her body without the towel lived up to the promise she thought she detected with it. After squaring her shoulders and tilting up her chin, she prepared to peel the towel away and was struck by the combativeness of her posture.

Why should she feel this reluctance to let the towel drop? Even the notion that she might do so caused her face to flame with color.

"Heavens!" she murmured. She wasn't all that prudish, was she? She was behaving like some Victorian maiden—which she damned well couldn't be. Not Victorian in these modern times and certainly, having been married to Garth, no maiden!

With all the strength at her disposal, she willed herself to lower the towel. She was dismayed to find she still couldn't do it. Something inside wouldn't let her. She grimaced disparagingly. Garth had teased her about her modesty, but this was ridiculous!

Was there something terribly wrong with her that was unsightly? She suddenly realized that while she'd never been aware that she was avoiding looking at her body when she was naked, this was precisely what she did. But even so, she'd seen enough to know that she had the appropriate quota of feminine accoutrements and that her parts were normally distributed. So she wasn't disfigured.

"This is stupid!" she cried, and her voice bounced back at her from the beige tile of the walls.

The problem had been blown up out of all proportion. It had become monumental.

"I'm going to bed." She announced her intention belligerently, as if there were someone there to stop her, but there was no one but her to hear the words she shouted.

Once in bed, she tossed and turned until she heard voices in the hall outside and the scraping of a key in the lock. Since he thought she would be sleeping, Garth had apparently prevailed upon the desk clerk to let him into the unit so he wouldn't have to disturb her.

When he entered, moving quietly about the room as he made his own preparations for the night, Julie remained very still, breathing deeply and evenly as she feigned sleep.

Garth is here and everything is going to be all right, she silently encouraged herself. This thought proved to be such an effective opiate that it was the last thing she was conscious of until she awoke before the sun the next morning.

Thanks to the length of time she'd spent in the regimen of the hospital, Julie no longer needed the chirrupy night nurse who would come into her room every day at the crack of dawn to waken her so she could scrub the sleep from her eyes in time to spend an hour or more waiting for the breakfast trays to be delivered to the ward. After having been subjected to four weeks of this, her inner alarm had gone off, and she opened her eyes promptly at six o'clock.

Garth was still sleeping soundly in the bed next to hers, and she envied him his undisturbed slumber. She lay without stirring, watching for daybreak in the minuscule amount of light the heavy weave of the drapes allowed to filter into the room.

The time seemed to drag until Garth finally woke up, but when he did, he was instantly alert and immensely vital. He literally bounded out of bed and immediately disappeared into the bathroom. Seconds later Julie heard the shower running and above this the sound of his voice raised in song, its volume amplified by the acoustics of the tub enclosure.

What was he singing? She listened with all of her being, and her mouth curved in a smile when she heard the western twang he'd adopted as he sang "Mamas, Don't Let Your Babies Grow Up to Be Cowboys." When several choruses of this were followed by "You Are the Sunshine of My Life," her smile became more generous, and when he broke into "Rocky Mountain High" for his finale, she giggled. He'd imitated the styles of Willie Nelson, Stevie Wonder, and John Denver and his impressions were so true to life, she expected half of the recording industry to come through the bathroom door behind him.

When he was dressed and had reentered the bedroom, it didn't take Julie long to realize that, notwithstanding his serenade from the shower, Garth was in a foul mood. His response to her good morning was a quelling stare, and when she'd had her turn in the shower and was ready for the day—dressed, much as he was, in jeans and a plaid shirt—her further attempts at conversation were met with equally dampening monosyllables.

She wondered whether he was always this out of sorts and uncommunicative first thing in the morning or if his grouchiness was due to their awkward situation. In some ways he was a victim of circumstances that were even less enviable than hers. How did he contrive to cope so coolly, trapped in the framework of marriage to a wife who didn't remember him? That, Julie thought, must be a much more bitter pill than the one she'd had to swallow.

Even after they were seated in the restaurant and he'd drunk his first cup of coffee, Garth's manner toward her did not sweeten. He was pleasant to their waitress; smiling and very courteous. It seemed to Julie that she was the only one who provoked his ill-tempered grumbles. In the end she, too, fell silent, and after a few bites of scrambled egg she merely crumbled her toast and pushed the food around on her plate.

"Aren't you going to finish that?" Garth asked sourly.

"I'm not very hungry."

His eyes roved over her, detached and critical as he conducted his assessment of her. "You look as if you haven't had a decent meal since you left California," he said.

So in Garth's opinion she was too thin, she thought, shrugging ruefully as she said farewell to her inflated estimate of her figure. "Well, you know hospital food," she replied. "You can tell the day of the week by the menu. It's so predictable, it's boring."

For a time after they resumed their journey, Julie occupied herself with watching the scenery. It promised to be another glorious day, though not as warm as the one before. They left the towns of Sage and Cokeville behind, heading toward the Salt River Range of mountains, and the highway began to climb more perceptibly. In whatever direction she looked, there was something to fire the imagination and please the eye.

When they passed a draw that was below the grade of the highway and Julie saw a horse-drawn canvas-covered wagon, she turned to ask Garth if he thought it might have been a chuck wagon, but after one short glance at him she changed her mind.

His eyes were gray and dark as slate—and as hard —rendering his expression more forbidding than ever. As if he knew she'd been about to say something, he put another tape on the stereo. After he'd adjusted the tuning knobs, the measured cadences of a Chopin nocturne filled the moody silence in the car.

Again Julie recognized the performing artist. It had to be Horowitz. Surely no other pianist could shade each nuance of the melody so poignantly and still maintain the fine balance between passion and bathos. It was becoming apparent that Garth had catholic tastes in music and, if one could rely on her familiarity with his selections, so did she.

Reluctantly she turned her eyes away from Garth. Thunderheads were massing above the mountain peaks far to the north, and she had the distinct impression that a storm was brewing inside the car that would rival any fireworks Mother Nature could cook up.

Though she tried not to, she couldn't resist stealing an occasional look at her husband. She thought he resembled some dark angel when he frowned at something he saw in the road ahead. Despite the warmth of the day, she shivered. She had the notion that being Garth's wife—really his wife—might be, for her, the most direct pathway to hell. But she had no doubt that if only he wanted to, he could make even that seem like heaven.

When they reached the summit of the Salt River Pass, Garth pulled into the parking area by the side of the highway and they left the car to stretch their legs. They walked along the ridge, gazing at the previously unnoticed face of Wyoming that was revealed to them from this vantage point.

A panorama of the rolling flanks of the mountains stretched out before them as far as they could see. It was a peaceful vista in variegated green, stimulating to the senses but so gentle to the soul that Julie felt a sharp pang of regret that, for practical purposes, she was seeing it alone.

But as if Garth felt as keenly as she did that it was somehow wrong to experience such sublime tranquillity and remain willfully hostile, as if he longed as she did to share it with someone, he touched the back of her hand. Although his touch might have been purely accidental, she responded by turning her hand into the encompassing warmth of his and he held her fingers tightly, almost painfully.

For a long time they stood side by side, joined as much by the similarity of their reactions to the view as by their clasped hands. And they did not let go of each other when at last they retraced their steps to the car.

Chapter Five

With each mile they covered now the terrain became more rugged, the descent from the pass more abrupt. Preferring a picnic at one of the wooden tables by the river to a meal taken indoors, they stopped at the 'carryout' window of a fast-food café in Afton to buy provisions for lunch.

It was noticeably cooler now that they were farther north. There was a crystalline quality about the air and the barest hint of a breeze whispered through the stately ranks of the pines, inviting the bronzy-orange leaves of the willows to dance and fly away with it.

Because she'd eaten so little at breakfast, Julie was ravenous and the fish and chips tasted like ambrosia —with the addition of malt vinegar, better than ambrosia, she qualified as she greedily ate every crumb of her portion.

They'd finished their food and were almost through with their drinks when, without warning, Garth announced, "Daniel Leeds is married."

Julie darted a look at his face. It was a model of inscrutability. Her eyes skidded away from him and she pretended an interest she no longer felt in the river rushing by their picnic spot.

"Is that supposed to be of some significance to me?" she asked.

"You damned well know the answer to that!" Garth exclaimed harshly.

"Why are you telling me now? Yesterday you refused to discuss it even though I wanted to. Today, because it happens to suit *you,* you resurrect the subject."

"I didn't bring it up out of choice, I assure you," he replied. "It simply seemed to me that you should be informed of the fact before you actually see him."

Steeling herself to look directly at him, she persisted, "But why tell me now—at this moment? Why didn't you tell me yesterday?"

"I only learned about it last night when I called Leeds to let him know I'd located you and that we're on our way to see him." With exaggerated patience, Garth explained, "I've only spoken to him once. That was shortly after you disappeared and our conversation was confined to my notifying him that you might be coming to Jackson Hole. A few days later he telephoned to let me know you hadn't turned up. He asked to be kept posted and I saw that he was, but I didn't speak to him personally—not on that occasion and not since then. I asked my administrative assistant to take on that dubious privilege and he handled all the subsequent communications with Leeds as well."

Garth paused to drink the last few swallows of his beer. He studied the empty can meditatively as he scraped designs over the trademark with his thumbnail.

"When I called last night, Mrs. Leeds answered." He shook his head disgustedly and crushed the beer can. "She sounds a good deal older than her husband," he remarked caustically.

"How do you know she was his wife?" she argued, taking his criticism of the Leedses as a personal insult. "Maybe she's his housekeeper. Maybe she's a friend or a relative."

Garth's mouth hardened to a cynical line. "Sorry, Julie, but she was speaking in such a low tone of voice, I could barely hear her and when I suggested we might have a bad connection she told me it was because she'd answered the call on the extension in their bedroom. And she said—and I'm quoting her verbatim—'Dan's in bed. He's been so worried about Julie that he's hardly slept in the past few weeks, so I'd rather not disturb him.'

"To top it all off, she invited us to stay with them. Even *you* will have to admit, the only thing all of that could possibly add up to is 'wife'!"

Julie's reaction to this indictment was a disdainful silence.

"Well?" Garth prompted when she offered no opinion.

"You've convinced me," she conceded.

"And?"

"And nothing. Zero. Zilch! It makes no difference to me because I don't remember Daniel Leeds. And even if I did, he could have *ten* wives for all I'd care. I don't believe there's anything more than friendship between us."

Garth's expression became more skeptical than ever and, stung by the calculating way he was looking at her, she asked, "Why would I marry you if I were in love with someone else?"

"I can think of several possibilities," he replied

steadily. "The most likely one is that you were unhappy with your limited role in his life and you reached the conclusion that there was no future in continuing an affair with a married man. You decided that you'd look out for number one and after your grandmother died you came to California to reduce the odds you might waver in your decision."

His mouth twisted into an unpleasant downcurve that was almost a sneer. "What it all boils down to, is that you married me for a reason as old as time—*money*!"

"I've never heard anything more absurd!"

"What's absurd about it?" he asked, purposely misunderstanding her. "I'm no Onassis, but I'm not exactly a pauper either."

Unable to remain seated at the table when she was fuming inwardly, Julie leapt to her feet and all but ran to the river's edge. She heard Garth's beer can rattle against the metal rim of the trash barrel before it dropped in and she was aware that he was close on her heels, but she kept her eyes determinedly fixed on the pebbly bottom of the streambed until he took her by the shoulders and forcibly turned her. He was annoyed by her obstinacy and nearing the end of his patience, and he shook her a bit in exasperation.

"I wish I could pound some sense into that hot little head of yours. For your own good, sooner or later you're going to have to face facts." The measured calmness of his voice was nullified by the severity of his frown. "It's fairly obvious that you have enough of a conscience to feel guilty about what you've done and that accounts for your amnesia. You must know that your doctors could find no physical cause for it. Perhaps if you accepted the truth about yourself, your memory would return."

"Heaven protect me from amateur psychologists!" she petitioned heatedly. In what she hoped was a withering tone, she asked, "Did you dream that one up all by yourself, or did you have some help?"

"It's my own idea," he acknowledged, "but Doctor Ziegler agreed with it."

"What Doctor Ziegler knows about human nature could be written in block letters on the head of a pin!" she retorted. "And let me tell you, Garth Falconer, you'll never convince me that I'm so mercenary that I'd be capable of marrying a man—any man—for money alone." The pitch of her voice had risen with the force of her anger and her fury overcame her caution as she added, "Furthermore, I don't think you've told me this out of an altruistic desire to help me. I think your motive was nothing more and nothing less than sheer, cussed egotism!"

"I'm willing to admit that I have my share of ego. What's wrong with that?" he countered evenly. "But as to my being driven by it—that's a case of the pot calling the kettle black!"

They were standing toe to toe, practically nose to nose, as if they were prize fighters squaring off in the ring. Her eyes blazed up into the accusing fire of his and his hands were intolerably heavy on her shoulders, yet he'd spoken with the same deceptive quietness as before. Julie thought his core of stillness, like the eye of a hurricane, masked a potential for cataclysmic destructiveness. She found it more frightening than if he'd bullied and blustered, but she would not permit herself the luxury of backing down.

"You—" She stopped and pulled sharply away

from him. She was stymied, at a loss for an adjective odious enough to apply to him. Inadequately, she cried, "You can take your advice and your insulting opinions and blow them out your ear!"

"Come, come, Julie!" he chided mockingly. "You can do much better than that."

Rising to the bait, she snapped, "You're insufferable!"

He was completely unscathed by her outburst. His posture was relaxed and easy, with his hands resting on his hips, and that she had succeeded only in amusing him became obvious when he laughed outright. This goaded her into a further display of temperament.

"Oooh!" she wailed. "A person can't win with you. It makes me want to stamp my feet and scream."

"So?" He arched a condescending eyebrow at her. "Don't let me stop you. Lord knows you never have before."

Infuriated by this additional taunt, she actually did stamp her foot. As soon as she gave in to the impulse, she was embarrassed that she'd indulged in such childish histrionics. In a turmoil of anger and shame and confusion, she spun on her heel to dash away from Garth and into the pines. When she heard him calling her name, chasing her, she ran even faster. She felt as though she were being pursued by demons and she left the trail to dodge in and out among the trees and crash headlong through the underbrush.

In truth, her flight soon approached the proportions of a nightmare. From every side, branches and thorns reached out to clutch at her, to pluck at her clothing, to tear at her hair and skin. In her distraught state of mind, even the trunks of the trees seemed to assume frightening shapes.

Initially the pounding of Garth's steps and the snapping of twigs breaking beneath his feet kept pace with her and this was the most alarming aspect of all. But somehow she managed to elude him until she tapped her reserves of stamina for an additional burst of speed.

Julie could not begin to estimate how far she had run before she slowed to a walk. She no longer heard Garth so close behind and she knew only that she could not go any farther. Her legs gave way and she collapsed to sit on a fallen log. Her lungs were burning with a need for air and her chest was heaving as she labored to fill them. Her heart thudded erratically beneath her breastbone.

After a time it struck her that these sounds were the only ones she could hear and she held her breath to listen for some sign of Garth, but there were only the trilling notes of birdsong and the drowsy hum of insects. Even the wind was still and the silence was ominous.

"Garth," she whispered. Her heart skipped a beat and again she was breathless, this time with foreboding. More loudly, she called, "Garth!"

When there was no answer, she began backtracking along the path she had made, stopping now and again to listen and call his name. She was becoming more panicky with each step she took and relief swept over her when she heard a faint sound of movement in the brush ahead.

"Ga-a-arth!" she shouted as loudly as she could and this time her cry was followed by a muffled moan. She rushed in the direction from which it had come. She was shaking with fear when she entered a sunlit clearing and saw him lying so deathly still on the ground. She ran to him and dropped to her knees at his side, one hand searching anxiously for his pulse.

"Garth," she sobbed brokenly, "oh, Garth! Are you hurt?"

His eyes opened and with blinding speed he grasped her wrist and pulled her diagonally across his chest. With the impetus of the same fluid motion, he rolled her over onto her back. Taken by surprise, she found herself pinned to the springy carpet of the forest floor by the full weight of his body.

For a moment she looked up at him, entranced by the gold-flecked green of his eyes. They were at the same time unfathomable and piercing. She recalled the facility with which he could divine her thoughts and, fearful of what her own eyes might reveal, she averted them to stare at the coarse curling hair that was just visible in the opening of his shirt collar.

"You louse!" she choked. "You were faking."

"Sorry to disappoint you," he drawled.

"If this is supposed to be some kind of joke, I fail to see the humor in it. You scared me half to death."

"It was no joke." Their eyes met again as she scowled at him. "You think *you* were scared! I was afraid you'd get lost or injured and how else was I to stop you?" Her scowl vanished and her expression softened as he made this admission. "God!" he exclaimed, "you run like a deer, and once you'd left the trail you had the advantage of size. You went straight through brush that I had to go around."

Although he had expressed concern for her well-being, his grip on her hadn't relaxed. He held her spread-eagled and his hands were like manacles about her wrists. In her discomfort, she stirred uneasily, feeling bruised and ill-treated. As she did so, she became intensely aware of the muscular length of his thighs resting intimately between hers, of the hardness of his chest crushing her breasts.

Suddenly there was an unbearable tension between them and in desperation Julie erupted into motion, renewing her struggles to escape him.

This time it was Garth who had not anticipated her attack and she almost succeeded in freeing herself. She derived some satisfaction from the fact that his breathing was nearly as heavy as hers when he finally managed to subdue her. His fingers tightened around her wrist, dwarfing it as they overlapped to measure its circumference.

"Damn, but you're strong!" he complimented her with grudging admiration. "For all that your wrists are about as big as matchsticks! Where do you hide all your muscles?"

His eyes wandered freely over her shoulders and arms and again she thrashed about, but this time her efforts were short-lived. He was prepared for such tactics and he controlled her easily.

"Get off me, you great heavy ox," she gasped. "I can't breathe."

"You've certainly changed your tune," he observed, showing a callous lack of sympathy for her plight. "You never used to tell me that—at least, not this early in the game." His actions contradicted his words, however, and he complied with her request, shifting slightly away from her and supporting the weight of his torso with his elbows.

No sooner had this been accomplished, than Julie had cause to regret her complaint. As a result of Garth's change of position, her shirt gapped open to the waist, revealing the full curve of her breasts.

Under the fire of his dilated gaze, she felt her face grow hot with embarrassment. The lacy bra she was wearing provided little protection from his bold inspection of her. Not only that, her body had turned traitor and her excitement was transparently clear. All he'd had to do was *look* at her and the rosy nipples had grown saucily erect.

"You've torn your shirt," Garth murmured thickly, "and you've hurt yourself."

Even as he pointed this out, she became aware of the sting of the scratch. In her mind's eye she could see, as he must, the droplets of blood that had been drawn by the thorn when it inflicted the wound, saw the way their redness emphasized the ivory pallor of her skin.

Her pulse clamored unevenly in the hollow of her throat and she felt strangely boneless. An alien heat and langour had invaded her limbs and she was caught up in the inevitability of whatever was about to happen.

Unable to stop him, not wanting to stop him, she watched as Garth lowered his head and touched his mouth to the scratch that marred the creamy flesh. With infinite slowness, he traced its jagged course with his lips while his fingers deftly released the fastening of her bra to bare her breasts completely.

She instinctively arched her back and her eyes ...akly when, at last, the sweet warmth of his ...ndoned the silkiness of skin to take posses- ...htly budded velvet of the nipple. Softly, so softly, he cherished it, coaxing it into full bloom with his tongue, savoring it with exquisite thoroughness.

Julie yearned to wrap her arms around him and draw him even closer to her, to hold him tightly and never let him go. The desire to prolong the tantalizing contact, to deepen it, was so urgent that she ached with the need to surrender to the demands of her body, but with some feeble residue of sanity she fought the compulsion.

Digging her fingertips into the bed of pine needles on which they lay, she concentrated on the discomfort caused by a pine cone that had lodged between her shoulder blades and was projecting its sharp spines into her back. She remained quiescent, neither resisting nor responding, as she battled to overcome the seduction of Garth's mouth, still lingering at her breast.

Within a matter of seconds, her hard won passivity became apparent to Garth. He raised his head and leaned away from her and she sensed that he was studying her face. Even now she was sick with longing for him and she gritted her teeth, resolving to keep her own eyes closed. But his fingers plowed through the tangle of her hair to curve insistently around the nape of her neck while his thumb tilted her chin, forcing her to confront him. Reluctantly she opened her eyes.

"I'm sorry," he apologized gruffly. "Resisting temptation may be good for the soul, but it's never been my strong suit."

Thinking that he probably hadn't had to exercise much resistance to temptation where women were concerned, thinking that they must fall into his

71

hands like ripe fruit, Julie replied shakily, "It's too soon."

"I know," he said.

"I wish—"

Garth looked at her quizzically but she was unable to continue speaking.

"I know," he repeated.

Did he? she wondered. Even she wasn't sure precisely what she wished.

He levered himself to his feet and pulled her up beside him so quickly that she felt light-headed. She leaned against him without self-consciousness, grateful for his matter-of-fact attitude as he adjusted her clothing and dusted her off.

"You have half of Wyoming in your hair," he quipped.

He began picking out the worst of the pine needles and leaves, the small pieces of bark and bits of moss. Her hair was thick and fine as thistledown, extending to several inches below her shoulders, and this took a long time. After several minutes had passed, she ventured, "It's so long and hard to manage, it's nothing but a nuisance. Maybe I should have it cut."

"No," he said sharply. "Don't do that."

With his pocket comb he gently removed most of the snarls. When he had finished, he stood back to survey his handiwork. She watched him circumspectly, not knowing exactly what to make of his solicitude.

He smiled briefly, indicating his satisfaction with the job he'd done, and slid the comb into the back pocket of his jeans.

"Are you ready to go?" he asked.

She nodded and he led the way back to the river.

Together they gathered up the debris from their picnic table and disposed of it. Before they left, she tried to bathe her face by the river and since the only mirrors available were those in the car, Garth even washed away the grime with a handful of tissues.

For some reason his tenderness made her feel like crying.

Chapter Six

It was dark when they reached Jackson, but even the brash forest of neon that exhorted the traveler to have his car serviced, to buy gifts and souvenirs, to eat, drink and make merry, could not completely disguise the uninhibited frontier flavor of the town.

They stopped only long enough to check into a motel and change clothes. While Julie tidied her appearance and slipped into the cream-colored pantsuit, Garth telephoned Daniel Leeds to advise him of their arrival and ask for directions to his home. When Julie came out of the bathroom, she found Garth was already dressed and was pacing restlessly while he waited for her to finish getting ready to leave.

The moment she returned to the bedroom he said, "Let's go. Leeds is married but he says he 'can't wait to see his darling Julie.'"

Julie was nonplussed by the tone in which Garth delivered the message from Daniel Leeds. The timbre of his voice had changed. It had become deeper, more intimate and almost melodic, with a smoky resonance. She puzzled over this as they drove along Broadway toward Cache Street.

That Garth had been mimicking Daniel Leeds was

obvious, and this led her to wonder, uncomfortably, whether she could have been mistaken in her assertion that there was only friendship between Leeds and herself.

They passed the crowded boardwalks of the town square, with its cluster of saloons and archways of elks' antlers, and shortly after this the lights of the town grew more widely spaced and finally disappeared altogether as they sped through the inky blackness of the night.

They had been driving for perhaps fifteen minutes when Garth eased back on the accelerator. Leaning slightly forward in the driver's seat, he began to peer more vigilantly at the roadside to their right. Ragged, wind-driven clouds scudded across the face of the moon, and the two of them might have missed the narrow track to the Leeds's property if the clouds hadn't thinned at an opportune moment. As it was, by the time Garth spotted the weather-beaten sign he'd been looking for, it was too late to make the turn.

He braked the car to a stop and, slamming into reverse, backed up until the headlights framed the signboard. It was mounted on a rusted metal post shaped like an inverted *L* and it swung in the wind with a screeching clangor. Once white, it had been scoured by the elements to a chalky gray, and the lettering on it had faded so badly that Julie could just pick out the name DANIEL W. LEEDS, D.V.M.

"He's a veterinarian?"

"Yes," Garth answered tersely.

The car spurted forward, Garth spun the wheel, and they left the highway for the lane. The tires of the car drummed over a metal cattle guard and

75

crunched over gravel. A single light beckoned them through the stand of trees ahead.

The house was sheltered by spruce and cotton-wood trees and bathed in a circle of illumination that emanated from a floodlight affixed to one of the out-buildings. It was a basic saltbox design with rustic wood siding, but for all its simplicity and despite the fact that its front windows were dark, there was a warm, welcoming quality about it.

Somehow Julie knew that this was the kind of house where casual callers went in through the kitch-en door to sit at a clean-scrubbed table. She knew that even unexpected visitors would be cordially re-ceived. And, should they want it, they would be served mugs of coffee or mulled cider and slabs of apple pie topped with cheese, or wedges of fudge cake fresh from the oven. Because of her intuitive knowledge about the friendliness of this house, her nervousness began to wane.

The rapid-fire staccato of a dog barking some-where inside the house greeted them when Garth parked the car in the cul-de-sac near the front walk. Without waiting for him to assist her, Julie opened her door and climbed out of the car. As she did so, a light came on in one of the front windows of the house, the door opened, and a woman stepped out onto the porch.

It was too dark to be able to distinguish her fea-tures, but the light escaping from the house showed her in silhouette. She was tall and lush-bodied. Sta-tuesque, Julie mentally qualified.

"Julie?" the woman inquired. Her voice was a surprise for it didn't go with her body. She turned toward the house. "Dan!" she cried excitedly over her shoulder, "Julie's here!"

The yelping of the dog had become louder, more frenzied. From inside a man's voice ordered, "Quiet!" and the barking stopped. In the next instant a streak of movement appeared behind the woman and the dog squeezed past her, erupting from the house to rocket across the porch and down the walk.

"Come back here, you damn fool dog!" called the woman and from the other side of the car Garth muttered an oath and launched himself in Julie's direction.

Julie watched the dog coming at her as if in slow motion. He was a good-size German shepherd, but as he hurtled toward her he seemed positively gigantic; all fearsome lolling tongue and sharp rending teeth. She was paralyzed by terror when the beast reached her and reared on his hind feet. His hot breath filled her nostrils and his front paws came down on her shoulders with such force that she staggered and would have fallen if the car at her back hadn't prevented it.

But the dog was whining now, she realized, and his tail was wagging. He began licking her face, so delirious with joy that he was practically wagging his entire body. From somewhere deep within her, there came a tiny isolated snippet of remembrance. She wrapped her arms about the shepherd's neck and buried her face in the rough, shaggy coat.

"Buck?" she whispered. "Oh, Bucky! It's so good to see you, fella."

Garth was ashen-faced. "My God! I thought—"

"It's too bad Buck got out," the woman said as she hurried down the walk. "He and Julie were always

77

such good buddies, we were afraid his welcome would be on the overpowering side."

"You were right about that," Garth replied dryly.

"I remember him, Garth," Julie softly disclosed. She gave a shaky little laugh that bordered on tears, and repeated, "I remember Buck."

"I'm sorry you were needlessly alarmed." The woman offered her hand to Garth. "I'm Jessie Driesen, by the way. And you must be Julie's husband."

"Garth Falconer," he supplied. "Julie has mentioned you often and with great fondness, Mrs. Driesen. And 'alarmed' is putting it mildly. My knees are still knocking!" He smiled at Jessie as they shook hands. "We're here to see Mr. and Mrs. Leeds."

"There is no Mrs. Leeds."

"But I talked to her on the telephone only last night." Garth's tone was mystified.

"You talked to *me,* Mr. Falconer." Although Jessie had spoken with emphasis, she was unoffended. "I've lived with Dan for more than thirty years, but we're not legally married. My first husband deserted me, but not before he'd convinced me I never wanted to marry again."

Closely shadowed by Buck, Julie had moved away from the car to join them and when Jessie turned so that the light fell on her face, Julie was startled to see that in spite of her youthful figure and sprightly step, Jessie Driesen was closer to sixty than fifty. Her astonishment must have been apparent because Jessie remarked, "You don't know me, do you."

Julie shook her head. "I'm sorry."

"Well, I'm going to welcome you properly just the same," Jessie declared. Her smile was kind, and she took Julie in motherly arms to give her a heartwarming kiss. "Now," she said briskly, affectionately linking her arm with Julie's, "shall we go inside so Dan can get a look at you? He'll have my hide for taking so long!"

If Jessie Driesen had been a surprise, Daniel Leeds was a revelation. He awaited them in the living room at the back of the house where he was seated in a wing chair with one foot propped on a hassock, his face reflecting the ruddy glow of the flames leaping in the fireplace nearby. He was a burly, barrel-chested man in his mid-sixties with hair made more sandy than red by the gray in it and all-seeing bright blue eyes. His gingery eyebrows were heavy and extended upward in tufts at the peaks, giving him an appearance of constant wonder.

"You'll have to pardon me for not getting up," he said when Jessie had introduced Garth. He indicated the crutches beside his chair. "It's nothing serious, merely painful—an attack of gout."

"Too much of the good life," Jessie interposed.

In the brightly lighted room, Julie was able to see that Jessie's hair, eyes, and complexion were varying shades of tan. She was plain-faced as well as plain-spoken, but she was nevertheless lovely in her tranquillity.

"Come here, Julie, and let me get a good look at you," Dan requested. His voice was beautifully modulated and richly textured. When Julie stood shyly before him, he took one of her hands in his. "We'll have to see if we can't restore that tricky memory of yours while you're here." He gave her hand an encouraging squeeze. "With the four of us

79

working on it, that shouldn't be too laborious a task."

His smile was indulgent as it rested on her. He turned to Garth and he became frankly amused. "Do you know," he confided with disarming candor, "I've never seen myself as a dirty old man, but I wouldn't mind being a sex symbol, so when Jessie told me you'd formed the opinion that I'd alienated Julie's affections, I didn't know whether to be offended or flattered."

"It made me damned angry," Jessie said astringently, "but I suppose you must have had good reason to believe such a thing. And Dan made me even angrier when he led you on the way he did when you called earlier this evening. How was he to know you might not do something drastic?"

"I could tell he wasn't the kind who'd go off the deep end," Dan said, defending himself.

"You know more than I do, then," Garth said wryly. He glanced uncertainly at Julie. "You don't know how close I came to doing just that! Especially when you admitted flat out that you love Julie and in the next breath said you were married."

"But we're not," Jessie denied. "Not legally anyway."

"You're my wife, Jessie, in every way that really matters." Dan was adamant. "And I do love Julie. She's like the daughter we never had."

"I won't argue with that," Jessie agreed. "I love her too. And I love you, Daniel Leeds, even if you are an old fool!"

There was a closeness between these two that was touching to see, Julie thought, in spite of Dan's raised eyebrows that seemed to ask Garth, What can you do with such a woman?

Dan and Jessie urged them to check out of their motel and spend the night. Because she felt a sense of kinship with them, Julie found the idea appealing, and Garth seemed happy enough to go along with the plan. He made the trip into Jackson to collect their luggage and when he returned, he found a defiant Julie waiting for him in the room they were to share.

"I'm not going to sleep in this room with you," she announced. The tender curve of her mouth was set in a rebellious line.

"Why not?" Garth asked. "We shared a room last night."

"That was different. There were two beds." A wave of her hand called his attention to the double bed with which this room was furnished.

Garth sighed wearily and shook his head. "Julie, I've no intention of moving into another room."

"Then I will!" She made a move toward the hallway.

"No, you won't." He stationed himself directly in front of the door and although his stance was nonchalant, his smoldering expression warned her that, should it become necessary, he would use force to prevent her leaving. "You're my wife, Julie," he said softly.

"I don't *feel* as if we're married."

"But we are and you'll only find it more difficult to adjust to the fact if you continually postpone the normal husband-and-wife intimacies."

Her shoulders slumped dispiritedly and he reminded her, "I gave you my word I wouldn't make any demands."

"You also said you're not very good at resisting temptation."

"Don't flatter yourself," he retorted coldly. "It's been a long day—a long *three* days since I left California. Hell, it seems more like three years! After chasing you over half the country, all I'm interested in is a good night's sleep."

Garth turned on his heel and stalked out of the room and, left alone, Julie sank numbly onto the side of the offending bed and buried her face in her hands.

It was disquieting to reckon with the fact that, aside from one brief and minor skirmish, she would offer no opposition to sharing both a room and a bed with him. Part of her had wanted the controversy to end this way—with Garth imposing his will on her. Did he know that? Was that why he was so confident she would comply with his edict that he could simply walk away from her?

Something cold and damp nudged her hand away from her face and she looked up and saw that Buck had wandered into the room. The dog was sitting as close as possible to her and his fine intelligent eyes conveyed the message that he sensed her confusion and that he sympathized with her.

Still weighed down by the burden of her thoughts, Julie absently reached out to scratch Buck behind the ears and pet the fawn and sable coat over his neck and shoulders. His tail thumped the floor, and when she would have stopped, he nudged her hand with his nose to set it moving again.

"All right, Bucky," Julie said, laughing. "You

win." She rose and together they went downstairs to the living room.

Dan had certainly developed the gift of his expressive voice to the fullest, Julie thought sometime later as she listened to him telling Garth how he'd happened to settle in Jackson Hole. It was after midnight and Jessie had long since excused herself and retired, but Dan had held Garth so spellbound that he'd forgotten how ready he was for "a good night's sleep."

As for her, she was too contented to move from her cozy spot near the hearth. She was half lying against a floor cushion, watching shadows cast by the fire dancing on the ceiling. Buck had curled up beside her and his head was a comforting weight on her lap, while the sound of the men's talking wove its magic around her.

"My father and I first came west in the early thirties," Dan recounted. "Dad fought in the trenches in World War One and he'd been a victim of mustard gas. He never recovered from that, and we were riding the rails, heading for New Mexico. We thought the desert climate might help his lungs, but by the time we got to Jackson Hole, he was too sick to travel any farther.

"It goes without saying that we were poor—and I don't mean just temporarily short of funds. Lots of people like to tell about how, during the Depression, they lived in a cold-water flat or a tarpaper shack in some shantytown, maybe even under a bridge or in a railroad tile. But hell's bells!"—Dan snorted derisively—"they don't know what *poor* is. Now my dad and I were really hard up against it. We were so poor, we were living in a *bush* !"

Garth's quick smile showed that he was not gullible enough to accept this claim at face value.

"Dad got to cadging drinks that winter. It was one of the coldest on record," Dan added, digressing, "but the winters here are always cold. To the natives, spring is just two weeks of bad skiing! Then one night when he'd gotten more than moderately blitzed, Dad crawled into the backseat of Bert Ransome's Model A to keep warm. The trouble was, old Bert wasn't any too sober himself and he drove all the way home without noticing anything unusual. To make a long story short, the exhaust on the car was faulty, and Dad was asphyxiated."

Dan shook his head sadly. "Poor old man," he said, sighing. "But I guess maybe he was better off out of it."

"What did you do then?" Garth asked. "You couldn't have been much more than—"

"I was fifteen. A homely, scrawny kid with nothing at all to recommend me to anyone. I was like some wild creature. I trusted no one and I lived by the rule of the jungle."

Dan stared ruminatively into the fire for a few moments. "That was when I met Julie's grandparents," he continued. "I never knew a finer man than Jim Ayers. He never turned anyone away from his door. Every hobo in the state knew where he lived and most of 'em stopped by for a free meal at one time or another. Jim used to say they might be angels in disguise." Dan paused to clear his throat. "When they made Jim Ayers, they broke the mold. And in her own fashion Elizabeth was a good woman. They were newly married, but they took me in when no-body else would have a thing to do with me and they put up with all my shenanigans till I got myself straightened out.

"Now, the reason I've told you all of this is so Julie can appreciate that her grandmother had her fine points. In some ways she was more charitable than most, but the truth is, she wasn't cut out for mother-hood. Not for marriage either." Dan chuckled. "Jes-sie put it in a nutshell one time when she said Elizabeth was happy as a spinster, damned miserable as a wife, and the merriest widow you ever saw."

"By 'merry' do you mean that she liked to play the field?" asked Garth.

"Lord, no!" Dan's eyebrows shot up. "Elizabeth had no use whatsoever for men. I never could figure out how she and Jim got together long enough to produce Julie's mother. No," he repeated, "by 'mer-ry' I mean only that she found her own company more rewarding than anyone else's. She had impossi-bly high standards, you see, and she was the only one capable of meeting them. She had no tolerance at all for human failings and since she was the only 'saint' around, that kind of tended to put a crimp in her social life."

Garth glanced at Julie. "I think I see what you mean," he said thoughtfully.

The fire had burned down to ash-covered embers, but an errant gust of wind caused a sudden shower of sparks to fly up the chimney. Buck raised his head and whined, got to his feet, stretched and yawned prodigiously. He ambled toward the back door, his nails clicking on the polished wood of the floor-boards.

"Should I take him out?" Julie asked.

"You can let him out on his own," Dan replied. "He'll come back as soon as he's made his nightly rounds."

Julie opened the door and Buck lifted his nose and sniffed the night air before he trotted outside.

"He's a fine animal," Garth observed as he watched the dog standing in the doorway.

"He's getting on in years," Dan said. "Julie and Bucky kind of grew up together."

Garth stifled a yawn with his hand and Dan looked at the mantel clock. "Look at the time!" he exclaimed. "You're too good an audience, Garth. Jessie will tell you, you shouldn't give me so much encouragement, or I'm apt to go on all night."

Dan turned to study Julie, who was leaning against the newel while she waited for Buck to return. The light from the fixture directly over her head shadowed her features and revealed that she was pale with fatigue.

"Why don't you and Julie go on up to bed," Dan suggested. "We'll have plenty of time to talk tomorrow. You do plan to stay on awhile, don't you?"

Garth had also turned to study Julie. After some deliberation he replied, "Yes, if it's all right with you and Jessie, I think we will stay a few days."

Chapter Seven

———————————

Julie was cocooned in a delicious warmth that would have been utterly delightful if it weren't for the leaden weight around her middle. She straightened one leg fractionally, reaching with her toes for the end of the bed. When she encountered Garth's ankle, she froze and awoke fully. Her eyes flew open but except for this she didn't move. She seemed not even to breathe.

She was lying on her side near the edge of the bed and Garth lay so close behind her that his quiet respirations stirred the hair at the nape of her neck. Their bodies were spooned together, with his knees tucked into the hollow made by her drawn-up ones. The heaviness around her waist was his arm. Thank God it was outside the blankets! She could feel his hand partially covering hers and by the dead weight of it she knew that Garth was still asleep.

Moving only her eyes, she looked down. His hand was very big compared to hers. His fingers were long, brown, blunt-tipped. It was an extremely capable hand, very masterful-looking even though it was relaxed with sleep. Even his fingernails looked strong. The soft contours of her mouth turned upward at the fancifulness of this notion.

Her eyes strayed over his wrist and forearm, studying them as intently as if she were a sculptor preparing to model them; measuring the substance of bone, the hardness of muscle, the agility of sinew, the suppleness of skin. If she really were a sculptor—or was it sculptress? she wondered—what material would she use for such a project?

She discarded the possibilities of clay, but asked herself, Should Garth's hand and forearm be cast in bronze in an attempt to duplicate his skin tones, or should they be chiseled from stone for firmness? No, she thought, neither of these was the right choice.

Perhaps they should be carved from wood. Something tough enough to have endured and flourished in spite of adversity would more nearly approximate the masculine vitality of such a subject. But what variety? Though the color wasn't right, it should be oak. She was sure about that.

And the wristwatch. It was only six thirty and the dial was barely visible in the dusky half-light. She looked at it closely and saw that it was a gold quartz model of an exclusive brand. She had no doubt it was as valuable as it was handsome, but it would definitely have to go.

She was distracted by the soft, dark hairs on his wrist, a few of which were caught up in the watchband. She thought he had just the right amount to be virile and sexy without looking brutish. Her fingers itched to touch it and she made herself look away. Her eyes roamed back to his hand.

Aside from the watch, he wore no jewelry, not even a wedding ring. She realized she was twisting the gold band on her own finger. In a number of ways she'd surprised herself this morning. The first surprise was that she'd slept at all the night before, the second was that she hadn't stolen out of bed as soon as she'd awakened, and the third was that she was wishing Garth would wake up too. And do what? she asked herself. The answer sprang into her mind, full-blown. If he were to move his hand just a little bit in either direction . . . The final surprise was the steaminess of the thoughts she was entertaining at this very minute.

Applying a brake to her wayward fancies, Julie said to herself, "I'll stay here for just a few more seconds and then I'll get up." She closed her eyes and snuggled her cheek into a more restful angle on the pillow. She was no longer bothered by the weight of Garth's arm around her waist; she welcomed it.

Maybe maple would be a better choice than oak, she mused, or maybe it should be walnut. And should Garth's hand be sculpted open or closed in a fist? She was still pondering this when she drifted off to sleep once again.

The next time Julie awoke, she cautiously opened one eye and determined that it was full daylight. She stretched out one arm and found that she was alone in the bed. Rolling to Garth's side of the mattress, she buried her face in the depression made in the pillow by his head.

She smiled when she heard him singing in the shower that adjoined their room. Who was he this morning? The walls in the house were sturdier than those in the motel, but she thought he sounded very much like Billy Joel.

For some reason this filled her with optimism, and she threw the covers back and jumped out of bed, grinning at her energetic start to the day. In the hospital she'd been prone to making a slower return to full power. Usually she tested the climate of the morning a little at a time, as if she were a swimmer trying to accustom herself to the coldness of the water by dipping a toe into it.

She went to the window, intending to have only a brief look outside, but the view of the mountains from this perspective deserved more than a cursory glance. They demanded more even than awe; they were worthy of veneration.

"My God," she breathed softly. How could she have forgotten about the Tetons? This morning their glacier-ravaged faces were concealed from the earth-bound valley at their feet by the clouds they had captured in their craggy peaks, but in spite of this they dominated the landscape, vaulting toward the sky as if they would lay siege to the gates of heaven itself.

When she saw the Tetons, Julie forgot that she was wearing only Garth's pajama top. She was still at the window when he came out of the bathroom.

"There's a sight that makes my trip worthwhile," he said.

She started, for she had been unaware of his return, and when she saw that he was looking at her instead of the Tetons, she became terribly conscious of her state of undress.

Garth wore only jeans belted low on his hips. There was a towel draped around his neck and he was using one corner of it to wipe away the traces of shaving lather that dotted his chin. Its whiteness made his smoothly tanned skin seem even darker. She'd been right about his build. He was lean-waisted and slim-hipped, and his belly was taut and flat, without an ounce of excess flesh. The muscles of his chest and shoulders were whipcord hard and they rippled with his slightest movement as he dried his face.

Julie realized she was staring and when she lifted her gaze, he raised one eyebrow as if to inquire whether she'd seen enough. Her cheeks stung hotly and she mumbled, "If you're through in the shower, I'll take my turn now." She didn't wait for his answer before she bolted for the bathroom.

Once there, she turned the water on and stepped under the spray without testing it. It was so cold, it took her breath away, and although she knew that it might be just the thing to cool her inflamed senses, she adjusted the taps until the water was comfortably warm. She'd forgotten her showercap, and when her hair got wet, she decided she might as well shampoo it. By the time she'd toweled it dry enough to secure it in twin ponytails and was dressed in jeans and yet another plaid shirt, Garth had come back upstairs to see how she was progressing.

"Jessie wants to know if you're about ready for breakfast," he said.

"I will be as soon as I finish making the bed," she replied as she pulled the bottom sheet tight and tucked the excess material under the mattress. Garth leaned one shoulder against the doorjamb and stood with his hands in his pockets, watching with more interest than her actions called for as she smoothed the top sheet over the mattress and mitered the corners at the foot.

"You could bounce a dime off that bottom sheet," he commented idly. "I haven't seen a bed made that way since boot camp. Did you learn to do that in the hospital?"

Without thinking, Julie replied, "No, I—" Her brows knitted in a frown. "I'm not sure where I learned it."

Garth pushed away from the door and came to the bed to help her with the spread. "Dan told me there's a trail to the Snake River on the other side of the highway," he said. He handed her one of the pillows. "Would you care to go for a walk after breakfast?"

"I'd like that."

She smiled at him and was disappointed when he only inclined his head in response. But when they left the room, he put his arm around her shoulders and he kept it there all the way downstairs until they reached the kitchen.

Dan advised them not to take the dog with them on their walk. "You won't see any game if Buck's along," he said. "Not that it's any fault of his. He's a gentleman; besides which, he's too old to go chasing after moose or elk, but they're just poor dumb critters and they don't know that."

Although they left the shepherd at home, they didn't see any sign of bigger game, but in one swampy area the trail skirted a beaver pond and when they'd reached the river, they saw some Canada geese and trumpeter swans.

An inflatable raft drifted by. One of the men in it was paddling desultorily and the other was casting for trout. They greeted them with smiles and silent waves of their hands.

Throughout their hike Julie had known that Garth was observing her expectantly, and when she caught him studying her as they sat on the riverbank, she exclaimed irritably, "I do wish you wouldn't keep watching me like that. If I recognize anything, you'll be the first to know!"

Garth grinned and reached out to tweak one of her ponytails. "That seems fair enough," he said. "It's just that there have been occasions when you haven't been particularly open with me."

"You're not exactly the town crier yourself," she returned lightly, grateful for the opening he'd given her. "For instance, don't you think it's time you told me why you were so positive I was in love with Dan?"

Garth nodded. "I felt like the worst kind of fool when I first saw him. I'd like to thank you for not rubbing it in."

She shrugged dismissively, but her eyes were troubled. "Am I the kind of person who gloats and says 'I told you so'?"

"Not usually, but I honestly couldn't blame you if you'd gloated a bit about this. I gave you a rough enough time over it." He sighed. "I'm not sure it's the wisest course, but I agree that you deserve an explanation."

Garth got to his feet and moved down the bank. He stood with his back to her, looking toward the cloud-obscured ridges of the Tetons.

"When we were dating, you spoke of Dan and Jessie with a great deal of affection, but you neglected to mention their common-law marriage and you never gave any indication of their ages."

"I can understand why I might not have," Julie offered defensively. "There's something ageless about them."

"At any rate you did make it obvious that you and Dan were much more than casual acquaintances and you were forever quoting him on one thing or another. In the light of subsequent events it seemed to me that you idolized him, and even before we were married, I thought the two of you had had an affair that had gone sour. But after you'd accepted my proposal, it never occurred to me that you might still be in love with him until after the wedding."

"But why? Was I—was I cold to you or something like that?"

"I never had the opportunity to find out."

"I thought—"

"I know what you thought," Garth interrupted sharply, "but the incident you dreamed about—the one on the beach—that happened on our wedding day. We were married in the morning and that same afternoon—" He stopped abruptly in midsentence.

The wind tore some leaves from the trees and sent them scuttling in dry, rattling cartwheels along the ground. Julie found she was shivering. Hugging her arms tightly to her sides, she wound them about her waist and slid her hands inside the cuffs of her sweater, trying ineffectually to dispel the chill.

"At the outset," Garth continued, "you seemed quite happy. You were a little edgy, but I attributed that to bridal jitters." He paused and shook his head.

"You didn't impress me as being frigid. We were in a little grottolike place back among the rocks and I wanted to make love to you. At first you acted as if you wanted it, too, but at the last minute you called a halt. You said you were afraid someone might come by.

"It seemed private enough to me but it was a

plausible excuse, given what I thought I knew about you. There had been times when you'd let yourself go and when that happened, you were incredibly responsive, yet you'd always retained a certain degree of . . . I don't know. Modesty, shyness, reserve—*something* that held you back. It was only afterward that I became convinced the real reason for your restraint was that you were still in love with Dan Leeds."

Julie moistened her lips. "Why?" she asked. "What happened?" She felt so cold now that her teeth began to chatter, and she had to clench her jaw to stop them.

"I went for a swim to cool off," Garth said. He was speaking rapidly. "You went back to our hotel room. By the time I returned, you'd left. You couldn't have had more than an hour's start, but you managed to throw me off the scent. You left most of your things behind along with a note that you were going for a walk. We'd been arguing on the beach, so I saw nothing out of the ordinary in that. It was typical."

On the last words his voice had grown bitterly abrasive, and she was struck by the rigidity of his spine, by the proud set of his shoulders. It made him seem strangely vulnerable, like a young boy who would not admit to feeling pain no matter how deep the hurt. This time, instead of being frightened by his pride, she wanted to go to him and take him in her arms. She wanted to offer him comfort, but she sensed that he would repulse such an attempt on her part.

His self-mastery was truly phenomenal, however. Within the space of a few seconds, he regained control and she could see the stiffness leave his back.

When he resumed speaking, his voice held no hint of censure, no anger. It was as impersonal as if he were discussing two strangers.

"It was another hour before I began to suspect you weren't coming back. I went out to look for you on the hotel grounds, and it was probably half an hour later before I questioned the desk clerk and some of the staff. Finally I got around to talking to the switchboard operator, and she told me you'd tried to make a telephone call to a party named Daniel Leeds in Jackson, Wyoming, but that she hadn't been able to put the call through for you.

"That's when I called Dan. He was concerned. Hell, he was frantic, really. And his voice conjured up the image of the matinee-idol type. What it all seemed to add up to was that you'd gotten cold feet and run back to your lover.

"I went through the motions of contacting car rental agencies, taxicab companies, and the airport. It never occurred to me to check the bus lines, and it wasn't till I'd arrived home the next morning that I thought to look in your suitcases. Sure enough, you'd left another note in one of them but it wasn't terribly informative. All you'd written was 'Forgive me.' "

Garth laughed sardonically and shifted his weight from one foot to the other. Although he was wearing no sweater, he appeared not to notice the iciness of the wind, even when a stronger gust outlined the powerful length of his thighs and plastered his shirt against his back.

"I didn't file a missing persons report right away," he said flatly. "After all, you'd left under your own steam and of your own volition. It wasn't till you hadn't shown up here and I'd had no word from you for a couple of weeks that I got around to that. The police weren't very enthusiastic about following up on the complaint, but they had to put out routine inquiries, and they struck pay dirt. The rest you know."

There was a silence that remained unbroken until Garth swiveled around to look at her. His expression was guarded.

"Well?" he challenged. "No questions? Don't you want to make some rebuttal to that long sad story?"

Julie shook her head and blinked back tears. "Only that I still hope you'll forgive me," she said.

This was not entirely truthful, for she badly wanted to know whether anything other than his pride had been wounded by her precipitate actions. Had he loved her? she wondered, but she hadn't the courage to ask.

Garth's eyes glinted gray-green with disbelief. "You've no desire to indulge in angry countercharges?"

"No," she replied huskily.

"Not one little insult?" he prompted. "No sarcasm?"

Again she shook her head. She had never seen Garth unsure of himself, but he was now.

"I think you've lost more than your memory," he muttered. "You're the lady who always lived by the rule that the best defense was a strong offense. Either you've undergone a radical change or you're putting on one helluva good act!"

"I don't understand. Would you prefer that I do those things?"

"No, Julie, far from it. I'm basically a peaceloving man."

Garth's eyes crinkled at the corners as he said this and when he tried to suppress his laughter so he could don his version of a serene expression, he failed miserably. Her frankly skeptical look only made him laugh all the harder, but when he noticed she was trembling, he sobered and held out his hands to pull her to her feet.

"You're cold," he observed gently. "You should have told me."

He chafed her icy hands with his, blew softly on them to warm them, dropped a quick kiss on the cleft in her chin, and planted another on the tip of her nose. Although the day was still cloudy and the wind had the feel of snow in it, Julie no longer felt cold.

Chapter Eight

———————————

Just across the hall from the kitchen was a formal dining room, but Dan and Jessie preferred to have their meals at a round oak table in a little ell at one end of the kitchen. The alcove had a picture window that looked directly into the woods; a pair of binoculars at the ready on the windowsill attested to the fact that they enjoyed watching the birds and animals and the changing seasons from this ringside seat.

As Julie helped Jessie prepare lunch later that day she noticed what a pleasant room the kitchen was. Its decor was a cheerful blend of dark-stained cabinetry, used brick, and gleaming copper utensils. Part of Dan's collection of Indian baskets was displayed here as were Jessie's wildlife prints.

Garth and Dan came in just as she and Jessie were putting the food on the table. When the men entered the dining alcove, Jessie called to Garth, "You're just the person I wanted to see." She held out a jar of olives. "Would you open this for me?"

"Sure thing," Garth said. After opening the jar easily, he handed it back to her.

Dan made his slow way to the table, his steps accompanied by the steady thump of his crutches. "I'll give you a little tip, Garth." He laughed and seated himself. "If you want to make your marriage last, there are three things you should never let Julie bring across the threshold of your house. One of them is a hairpin, another is a metal nail file, and the last is one of those little gizmos that clamps onto a jar lid to open it."

Garth was puzzled. "I'm afraid I miss the point."

"A good-looking woman can always find a man to warm her bed and father her children," Daniel theorized solemnly, "and she can repair anything that's broken with a nail file and a hairpin. If she figures out some way to open jars too—well, what does she want a husband for? He's obsolete!"

Jessie laughed with Dan. "You sure walked into that one, Garth."

"How about it, Julie?" Garth asked. "Do you agree with Dan's philosophy?"

"I can open jars myself, thank you," she replied absently as she carried the tureen of soup to the table.

Garth held Julie's chair for her and smiled wryly at Dan above her head. "She can too. Don't be fooled by her fragile appearance. She can practically bend steel bars with her bare hands."

Dan was suddenly sober. "I'd forgotten about that," he said.

"Me too," Jessie concurred thoughtfully. She turned to Garth. "You know how she got to be so strong, don't you?"

"No, I don't," Garth answered shortly. "Did she used to lift weights or something?"

Jessie sniffed disgustedly. "She used to lift Elizabeth. Heaven knows she was a dead weight on the poor girl."

"Now, Jessie," Dan murmured soothingly.

"Okay, okay, I'm sorry," Jessie apologized brusquely. "What I actually had in mind is that Julie was once a fine gymnast. She used to be able to do all sorts of acrobatics on those funny uneven bars and everything."

Dan nodded. "That's right, Garth. Her coach thought she showed enough potential that he arranged for her to have a scholarship to attend a special school where she'd get concentrated training in gymnastics. He'd coached champions before, so I guess he knew what he was talking about."

"So what happened?" Garth asked.

"Her grandmother's stroke," Jessie replied. "Julie was all set to go, but when Elizabeth got sick, she wouldn't think of leaving her."

Garth looked at Julie as if he were seeing her anew. "I didn't know," he said slowly. "Julie never told me about that."

"I can't say I'm surprised to hear it." Dan smiled gently at the younger man. "I get the impression that you don't really know Julie very well."

"No," Garth admitted. "I'm beginning to realize that fact more every day."

Dan eyed his vegetarian fare with distaste and cast an envious glance at the lamb chops the rest of them were having. Because he was troubled by gout, he was allowed a very limited amount of meat. He sighed resignedly and sampled his spinach soufflé before he set about filling in the gaps in Garth's knowledge. "As I told you last night," he said, "Julie's grandmother wasn't the motherly type. She was too inflexible."

"That's putting it mildly," Jessie interjected.

"At the same time," Dan continued as if he hadn't

been interrupted, "she was a perfectionist, and the upshot of this was that she overcompensated. Her way of dealing with any failure on Julie's part to live up to her expectations was to clamp down even harder."

"What Dan's trying to say is she would have made a great drill instructor," Jessie contributed. "But a five-year-old girl who's just lost her parents is not a Marine recruit."

"Now, Jessie," Dan said, repeating his mild reproach. "Elizabeth wanted to do the right thing." Jessie opened her mouth to make another comment and Dan said firmly, "I admit that because of her kindness to me when I was a boy, I don't see her in as unflattering a light as you, but please try to remember it's Julie's grandmother we're discussing."

Jessie speared a bite of salad with her fork and chewed it in thoughtful silence. "You're right, Dan," she agreed. "For all that woman's shortcomings Julie loved her."

Dan nodded. "She tried to please Elizabeth," he said to Garth, "but it was like trying to make water run uphill. Like most children, Julie was naturally inquisitive. She wanted to try new things, and the more Elizabeth restricted her, the harder she fought it. Elizabeth never recognized that it was her own overprotectiveness that incited Julie to become more and more reckless.

"Julie's coach believed one reason she showed such promise in gymnastics was a result of her willingness to try anything, and that was largely because she'd been forced into taking that attitude. She had to climb higher, run faster, swim farther—"

"I think I understand," Garth remarked. "Not

long after Julie and I met, we happened to go to a beach that was popular with the hang-gliding crowd. By the end of the day, Julie had advanced from the beginner's level to the intermediate's, and she'd have attempted a flight from the highest one if I hadn't talked her out of it."

This can't be me they're talking about, Julie thought. Her feeling of unreality grew as Dan told Garth about some of the deceptions she'd practiced in order to circumvent her grandmother's rules without resorting to actual lies.

"She'd observe the letter of Elizabeth's laws, but not the spirit of them," Dan revealed. "She was about as resourceful as they come."

"How do you mean?" Garth probed.

"Well, for example there was a gully near the grade school where the local kids made what they called a pig swing. What it consisted of was a length of rope with a board tied on at one end in a sort of bosun's-chair arrangement. They'd tie the other end to a big spruce and swing out over the gully on it." Dan chuckled. "The pig part referred to the fact that if they happened to fall off after a rain, they'd get so danged muddy.

"Elizabeth was horrified when she came to pick Julie up after school one day and found her taking a turn on it. I guess she had some justification because the gully was pretty deep, but kids being what they are, they were all doing it. Nevertheless, she ordered Julie not to swing on it, and Julie gave her word she wouldn't. And she didn't. What she did instead was far more hazardous. She took on the chore of shinnying up to the top of the tree to tie the rope!"

He paused to help himself to another corn muffin before he went on. "There was another occasion when Elizabeth forbade Julie's taking part in a class outing that involved rafting down the Grand Canyon of the Snake River. Julie promised she wouldn't set foot in the excursion raft, but she tried to make the trip in a jerry-built rig she'd put together with baling wire. The doggone thing started breaking up almost immediately, and by the time she'd gone through the first stretch of white water, she was clinging to a single piece of driftwood."

Everyone laughed, including Dan, but when their laughter had abated, he said, "It's funny now, but I don't mind telling you it was hair-raising at the time. And even more dangerous than that was the time when Elizabeth refused to give Julie permission to sign up for a course at the mountaineering school and she set about teaching herself the rudiments of rock-climbing and rappelling. I'll never figure out how she survived that little escapade. The cardinal rule around here is that you *never* climb alone."

Julie could not imagine engaging in such exploits, and her expression had become increasingly doubtful.

"Why do you look so dubious?" asked Garth.

She shook her head. "It's hard to believe that I did those things. I don't feel all that adventurous and frankly it's frightening just to hear about them."

"You may not have felt any bolder when you were doing them," Garth said quietly. "For some people the only way to deal with fear is to deny they're afraid by forcing themselves to meet it head-on."

"Is that what prompted you to become an auto racer?" she asked softly.

"There are certain parallels," Garth replied, "but the risks you take in racing are calculated and it wasn't racing I was afraid of. It was boredom."

"Boredom!" Jessie cried, and Garth nodded. He drank some of his coffee before he continued.

"Before I'd reached my mid-twenties, I'd discovered what a mixed blessing it was to have been born into a privileged family. Things had always come my way too easily, and I was fresh out of new worlds to conquer. I thought I'd done it all."

His mouth quirked humorously, and he looked from Dan to Jessie as though he were gauging their interest. Both of them were listening as attentively as Julie.

"When it came to leading a pleasure-seeking existence, the fact was that I had done just about everything that wasn't outright felonious. As for the future, it threatened to be more empty than the present. All I could foresee was an endless search for bigger and better thrills, and they were getting harder to find and none of them lasted anyway." He grinned, mocking his youthful conceit.

"If all of this sounds cynical and melodramatic," he said dryly, "it's because it was. And so was I at that age. Of course what I really wanted to do wasn't at all dramatic. I wanted to go into the family business, but my father was understandably reluctant to entrust me with responsibility. Even if I hadn't had a wild and misspent youth, I doubt that he'd have allowed me any real input into the way things were run. I had a good deal of respect for Dad, but his greatest failing as a corporate manager was that he was hidebound by tradition. He saw no need for innovation. If a certain policy had been in effect when he'd assumed control of the company from his father, he stuck to it—even if it could be demonstrated that a new approach would be an improvement."

Garth fell silent as he held out his coffee cup to Jessie for a refill.

"So you went into racing," Dan remarked when Garth did not continue his narrative.

"Like a drowning man clutching at a straw," Garth said. "I'd never felt as *alive* as I did when I was driving in a race." He'd spoken flippantly, and Julie suspected that this was a cover for the intensity of his feelings.

"And now you run Falconer Construction," Dan said.

"It's Falconer Engineering Consultants these days —the firm rarely enters into construction contracts since I took over—but yes, I do run it with the help of a fine management team. Julie's uncle, Rupert Hastings, is our vice-president in charge of design."

"I used to wonder why Rupert and his wife didn't petition the court for custody of Julie after her parents died, or at least keep in touch with her."

"There had been a falling out between the two couples," Garth replied. "You must have heard about the scandal involving Julie's father."

"Oh, yes!" Jessie exclaimed irascibly. "We heard about it, and heard about it, and *heard* about it, ad nauseam, from Elizabeth."

"What scandal?" Julie asked quickly.

She had been listening to their conversation so quietly that the other three seemed to have forgotten about her and now, in unison, they realized their oversight and turned startled faces toward her. No one answered for a time. Their glances shied uneasily away from her to shift back and forth to one another in a kind of conspiracy of silence.

"Let it go, Julie, *please*," Dan pleaded. "Don't stir up all that old misery."

"What scandal?" she repeated. Her eyes were fixed on Garth, targeting her question directly at him.

"Your father was also employed by Falconer's, Julie," Garth answered as if he were carefully choosing his words. "He was the chief engineer on a bridge project in southern Oregon. Within a month of its opening, the bridge collapsed and an investigation showed that the material used by one of the subcontractors was below specifications. The company was held accountable for civil and punitive damages—three people had been killed when it collapsed—and your father was found guilty of accepting a bribe from the subcontractor to guarantee his approval of the substandard work."

Dan and Jessie exchanged an anxious look. Julie's face was strained, and so completely drained of color that it seemed all eyes. Her hands were tightly folded in her lap, and she held herself stiffly, as if to keep from flinching. Though Garth hadn't raised his voice, his words had struck her like blows, and she felt wounded by them.

"My father did that?" she whispered.

"No, Julie, he didn't." Garth covered her hands with one of his and he could feel her relax as he spoke. She slipped one hand confidingly into his, and as his fingers closed around it he marveled that something so delicately boned should be capable of such strength.

"Eventually he was cleared," Garth said. "It was unfortunate that it wasn't until after his death, but new evidence came to light that proved his assistant was the guilty party. Your father's only mistake was delegating too much authority to the man who sold us out." She clung to his hand with renewed pressure. "Your grandmother was notified of this development when it happened."

Dan and Jessie were gaping with amazement. "Elizabeth told us every detail about Ted Hastings's conviction," Jessie muttered, "but there wasn't a peep out of her concerning his exoneration."

This time Dan did not defend Elizabeth Ayers. "Why didn't Rupert contact Julie after Ted was acquitted?" he asked.

"I just don't know the answer to that," Garth returned. "A number of years had passed and in the interim Rupert had more than his share of family problems. Charlotte, his wife, is something of a shrew. On her own she can cause enough turmoil to keep half a dozen men occupied." He shrugged casually. "It's pure conjecture on my part because I was away at school most of the time when all this was going on, but Charlotte was once engaged to Ted, and I think she was jealous of Julie's mother. She might have discouraged any effort of Rupert's to win custody."

Sighing, Jessie got to her feet and began stacking the dishes. "This topic of discussion is likely to lead to enough indigestion to send bicarbonate of soda stocks soaring," she declared. "Let's talk about something more pleasant."

"Good idea, Jess," Dan agreed brightly.

Garth was relieved. "Tell me more about Julie," he requested. He was still holding her hand under the table, and she hated to have to free it when she rose to help Jessie serve dessert.

Dan willingly obliged, regaling Garth with anecdotes about Julie's childhood and adolescence. "We didn't see much of her once she'd finished high school," he revealed. "By then Elizabeth was failing so badly, Julie was pretty much tied down looking after her."

His compliments, augmented by Jessie's, grew more flowery, his commendations more fulsome, until Julie felt like screaming that she couldn't possibly be the angelic person they were describing. Instead she complained tartly, "I wish you wouldn't talk about me as if I'm not here. Even if my memory was functioning, I don't think I'd recognize myself. All this praise—it's too much! You'd think I was dead and you two were delivering my eulogy."

This time they allowed her to have the last word, and conversation turned to other things.

After lunch Dan invited Garth to his workshop for a demonstration in the art of tying flies. He was an enthusiastic angler and had years of experience in making his own lures.

"I have one little beauty you're going to love," Dan told Garth when he learned the younger man had enjoyed the limited amount of fly-fishing he'd done. "It's my personal favorite and it's surefire. Trout practically jump into your creel to get at it!"

"That's the last we'll see of them for a while," Jessie forecast good-naturedly when they left the table. "Now that Dan is semiretired, I see less of him than I did when he was working full-time. He's either in his shop or out on the river trying out his inventions. I swear, if I'd agree to serve his meals in there, he'd just move into the shop."

When they had finished clearing the table and loading the dishwasher, Julie asked, "Can I help with anything else?"

"I'd planned to bake some pies for the Autumn Festival the local women's club is sponsoring," Jessie replied. "You can peel the apples for me."

They worked together companionably, and when the pies were in the oven, filling the kitchen with delectable spicy aromas, Jessie made some coffee for the men, and Julie took it into the shop for them before she returned to the kitchen for tea.

"They were so deep in a discussion about a 'Number Four Brown Hex,' whatever that is, they hardly noticed me," Julie said. "Do you think they'll know the coffee is in there?"

"Never fear. I don't know about Garth, but Dan can smell coffee a mile away if he's upwind of it in a gale!"

Julie smiled at the picture this brought to mind, but she was stirring her tea with unnecessary care and Jessie thought she seemed preoccupied.

"There's something I'd like to ask you," Julie confessed hesitantly, "and I'm not sure there's any tactful way to do it. I wouldn't want to impose on your friendship."

"In other words you're afraid it might put me on the spot." Jessie reached out to pat Julie's hand. "Lord, child! From those pink cheeks of yours, I'd say you're the one who's uneasy. Ask away. If I don't want to answer, I'll tell you straight out, it's none of your business."

"It's—well—it's apparent you and Dan have very

110

different opinions about my grandmother. I just wondered why you disliked her."

"Mainly because she tried to poke her nose into our business," Jessie replied evenly.

"How do you mean?"

"When I first moved in with Dan, she started some ugly rumors about me. Until I settled her hash, she conducted a one-woman campaign to either run me out of town or undermine Dan's trust in me so he'd send me away."

Jessie's sharp-eyed glance took in Julie's apologetic expression, and she cautioned, "You understand I've told you this in confidence. Dan never found out who was behind all the gossip, and I could never bring myself to tell him and destroy his high regard for Elizabeth. It would have served no purpose, and he'd have been terribly hurt."

Julie nodded soberly. "Naturally I won't tell anyone. But what possible reason could my grandmother have had for doing such a thing?"

Jessie's face was contorted by a rueful grimace. "Elizabeth dearly loved to try and run other people's lives for them, and that was all the reason she needed. She saw everything in black and white and was so set in her belief that only she was equipped to judge the right and wrong of things, you'd have thought she had a direct line to God!"

As if to mitigate Elizabeth's culpability out of consideration for Julie, she added philosophically, "Of course, you have to remember that Elizabeth's sense of morality was outraged. She grew up in a time when it was commonly thought that sex outside of wedlock was a mortal sin. And even a married woman was expected to look upon sex as a duty and grin and bear it—and she'd better not grin too much either!"

Jessie's eyes twinkled mischievously. "That just goes to show you how society can sometimes carry its taboos too far. Sometimes individuals can, too, and so far as I'm concerned, that was Elizabeth's greatest failing. She couldn't understand that in loving each other as we do, Dan and I have hurt no one—and we've made each other very happy. I never could see any cause for shame in that."

Jessie had spoken quietly, without a trace of rancor, and when she paused to drink some of her tea, Julie was impressed once again by her tranquillity. Every aspect of her demeanor testified to the sureness of her inner peace. She exchanged an eloquent glance with Julie over the rim of her cup before she replaced it in its saucer.

"From the smell of those pies," she declared as she pushed her chair away from the table, "I'd say they're about finished baking."

Chapter Nine

With a poor imitation of being uncommonly fatigued, Jessie and Dan excused themselves and went to their room shortly after supper that night, leaving Garth and Julie alone in the living room.

"I'm surprised they didn't take poor old Buck with them," Garth quipped when the dog claimed his customary place next to Julie, with his head resting in her lap.

"I'm sorry they were so obvious," Julie said.

"Don't be embarrassed, Julie. And for God's sake don't apologize for Dan and Jessie. I'll admit I don't need to be hit over the head with a club to know how they expect us to occupy ourselves tonight, but I like them—partly because they are so transparent. You're lucky to have such staunch allies in your corner."

He was standing by the hearth, looking down at her, and he couldn't miss seeing the color that suffused her cheeks. He laughed softly and indicated the logs in the fireplace.

"Let's at least try to live up to their romantic ideal," he suggested.

"It would be a shame to let a ready-made fire go to waste," she agreed happily.

Garth sat on his heels and touched a match to the newspaper cones that were heaped beneath the logs in the grate. Dropping down beside her to share the floor cushion, he watched as the flames spread and leaped and, with a sudden rushing sound, licked voraciously at the wood, setting it ablaze.

As Julie stared into the flames she experienced once again the dizzy, disorienting feeling of being trapped in a timewarp. Her feeling of contentment vanished, dispersed by anxiety that threatened to expand into panic of unbearable dimensions. Though she tried to keep them open, her eyes closed, and the pungent sweetness of wood smoke became acrid and eye-stinging. The gentle warmth on her face became intense heat that surrounded her and would soon consume her. The cheery hissing-popping noises made by the pitch igniting in the wood became a deafening, all-encompassing roar. More than anything else, it was the sound that frightened her.

She was sobbing, but her eyes were dry—for she was too terrified for tears. Somewhere glass was breaking and someone was shouting her name. The voice was familiar and yet, somehow it was different . . . younger, not as deep. She wanted to run toward the voice and discovered she was unable to move her feet. She wanted to answer the shouts, but she couldn't. Her throat was too sore, too irritated by smoke.

A scream tore at her vocal cords, and when she hastily opened her eyes, she was surprised to find that no sound had escaped her. Garth was holding her close in his arms and she was safe.

"Shhh, it's all right now, Julie," he murmured

soothingly. She was shaking with fear, and he repeated, "It's all right."

"Yes," she replied dully. "It's gone now."

"Your parents died in a fire. Your house was completely destroyed. It was almost totally engulfed in flames before anyone even turned in the alarm."

"Someone rescued me," she said.

"Yes," he confirmed.

"Was it you, Garth?"

He nodded. "I managed to get to you by breaking in through your bedroom window just before—" He left the sentence unfinished but continued talking because it appeared to be having a calming effect.

"It was an odd coincidence, but the only reason I happened to know which room was yours was because I'd delivered some papers to your father that afternoon. You took quite a fancy to me. In fact you made such a pest of yourself that I finally joined you and your collection of dolls for a tea party to get you off my back. That was quite a blow to the macho image I tried to cultivate when I was sixteen. I had myself more than half convinced that I was twice that age and a ringer for Charles Bronson before you came along and ruined it all."

"Was I an awful nuisance?"

"Terrible," he said dryly.

Her trembling had ceased, and she lay limply against him with her head on his shoulder. He shifted his position slightly to cradle her more fully in his arms and pulled off the clasps that confined her hair. It reminded him of fine, dark silk as he ran his fingers through it to loosen it, and when he had finished, the soft fragrance of it clung to them—the scent of spring flowers.

"I'm sorry you had to remember the fire," he said. "It was a nightmare."

"Yes," she whispered. "Sometimes it's better not to remember."

His arms grew taut about her. "Why do you say that? Did you recall anything else today?"

She shook her head. "Only the way the sun sets behind the Tetons." His arms gradually relaxed, and she sighed deeply. "I wish I knew more about so many things."

"Such as?"

"My uncle. It's strange to know so little about my father's brother."

"You were never well acquainted with him, Julie."

"Because of the scandal?"

"No," he said thoughtfully. "I think it was mainly because of Charlotte. She's a very domineering woman and Rupert—well, Rupert is a good man, a kindhearted man, but he's no match for her."

"He's weak?"

"As far as his wife is concerned, yes, he is," Garth answered. "He's an easygoing guy, and Charlotte has raised bitchiness to the level of a fine art. Whenever she's thwarted, she goes straight for the jugular. I suppose, out of sheer self-preservation, Rupert no longer even tries to oppose her."

"Is that why Diane looks so unhappy in the wedding picture?"

"No," he said curtly.

"Then why—"

"She was recovering from an unhappy ending to a love affair at the time."

His arms still held her but he seemed remote.

When she moved a little away from him, he released her entirely and she felt lonely.

"Was her affair with you?" she asked tremulously.

"No!" For a moment he was taken aback. "What in God's name made you think that?"

"Diane is very lovely, but she looks so sad in the picture," Julie replied. His expression remained stony, and she added weakly, "I just thought she might have been in love with you."

"Well, you thought wrong," he emphasized coldly. "I won't try to kid you that I've been celibate. I haven't reached the age of thirty-four without having been involved with a few women. In the years before I took over Falconer Engineering, there were more than a few. But there has *never* been anything more than friendship between Diane and me."

Garth jumped to his feet and stalked the width of the room and back before he stopped, standing with one elbow propped on the mantel to glower down at her. A vein throbbed angrily in his temple.

"Dammit, Julie," he exploded. The side of his fist came down forcefully on the mantel. "Diane's like a sister to me!"

No sooner were the words out than his angry scowl was replaced by his boyish grin, and he relaxed, sitting on the hearth with his long legs sprawled out in front of him.

"Now I know how you must have felt when I accused you of being in love with Dan," he admitted sheepishly.

Julie's laughter was as carefree as if she'd been relieved of a huge burden, but when Buck's nap was disturbed by her fit of giggles, he lifted his head, got stiffly to his feet, and moved to Garth's side of the

117

fireplace, where he showed his teeth in a conciliatory grin before he settled down again with his head on Garth's thigh. The bemused, vaguely disbelieving way Garth watched this transference of affection was touching.

"I may find it hard to sympathize with you, but apparently Buck doesn't," she teased. "If it's any comfort to you, he's a very discerning animal."

"So he is," Garth remarked, returning her smile. "I must say I admire his taste too!" He stroked the shepherd's grizzled head. "When I was a kid, I always wanted a dog."

"Do you have one now?"

"No. My work takes me away from home too much for that to be practical. Dogs need a closer companionship with their owners than I can provide."

"How long have you been in charge of your company?"

"About three years."

"Mrs. Jenkins said you'd taken control when your father died."

Garth nodded. "Things were in bad shape at that time. There'd been a sharp cutback in highway programs and other construction, and Dad had some archaic theories about how the business should be run. He hadn't kept up with the latest advances in design and engineering either. What really kept the firm afloat was the momentum my grandfather had provided."

"Do you find your work as absorbing as you'd hoped it would be?"

"So far," he replied, shrugging with a nonchalance that, like his earlier flippancy, seemed false. "I certainly can't complain that I'm not challenged by it. We've branched out considerably. We do more consulting for private industry now than for public agencies—pipelines, power plants, that kind of thing. The company is back on its feet financially. Your uncle, incidentally, has been very effective at scouting out new clients for our services."

For a time they were silent, each of them diverted by the dying glow of the fire. Garth's face was partially shadowed, and this accentuated the austerity of his features, the pride that was so essential a part of him. Garth continued to pet Buck, and the dog's expression was almost human. Buck looked as if he were inordinately pleased with himself.

"In your own way," Julie surmised, "I think you're every bit as committed to the preservation of certain traditions as your father was."

After considering this briefly, Garth said, "I suppose that's true."

"Then why do you try to disguise the way you feel about your family heritage, about the work you do?"

"Haven't you heard?" he drawled. "The most important thing of all is to keep your cool."

"What kind of answer is that!"

"It's the *only* kind you're going to get until you have some confidence of equal value that you want to barter for a better one."

For a moment she was dumbfounded. Then, ignoring her misgivings, she blurted heedlessly, "I already have something to tell you. But I'll only trade it for the truth." She forced herself to meet his eyes squarely. "Is it a deal?"

"Why not?" Garth grinned broadly and cautioned, "It had better be good though."

The warning was cause for second thoughts, but she had gone too far for a graceful retreat and she had no desire to provoke further dissension between them. She inhaled deeply and announced in a shaky voice, "I think I'm falling in love with you all over again."

Now it was Garth who was speechless. His face was stunned and dark with some emotion she could not define, and she averted her eyes. She was appalled by her foolishness and she wasn't sure she wanted to hear his response.

He stood up so rapidly that he alarmed Buck, and the dog skittered away from him in confusion. He patted the shepherd on the head and said evenly, "That's okay, fella."

In the same quiet tone he declared, "It's late. I'll put Buck out and take care of locking up while you get ready for bed."

Moving automatically, Julie rose and walked blindly toward the stairs only to be stopped by his hand on her shoulder when she reached them.

"Good night, Julie," he said firmly, making it painfully clear that he would not be joining her in bed for anything other than sleep. He gave her a chaste kiss on the forehead and when she couldn't resist the impulse to lift her mouth for a more satisfactory caress, his hold on her tightened punishingly.

"Damn," Garth muttered, and in the next instant his arm hooked around her neck to propel her roughly toward him while his free hand threaded through stopping to grasp a handful and crush it fingers. When the unexpectedly savage mouth on hers forced her head back, wedged in the crook of his elbow.

120

He ground his lips into hers so fiercely that his beard grated her skin, and she went stiff with surprise at the first touch of his mouth but she sensed that his anger was directed as much at himself as at her; in spite of his roughness her lips softened to offer a timid response. And when her lips softened, so did Garth's, while becoming, at the same time, more demanding. Julie was hazily aware that she had only thought he'd kissed her before, for this time there was no holding back.

Garth's lips moved hungrily over hers, compelling her mouth to open for him. But no force was necessary. Her lips parted freely, wantonly. She was eager for the first heady contact of his tongue with hers, and when it came, his assault was softly insistent. Then he probed more intimately, and his ever-deepening invasion of her mouth assumed such a sweet urgency that she felt herself dissolving in the heat of his kiss and knew that nothing would ever be the same again. Surely she would be forever transformed in the fires generated by his passion.

Her arms were tightly linked around his waist and when his mouth left hers, she slid one hand upward over his chest to stroke his cheek with wonder; lightly tracing his earlobe, the spare angle of his jaw, the strongly defined arch of an eyebrow. His eyes were dark green with amber flames scintillating in their depths.

"You have the sexiest eyes," she murmured, and Garth's pupils expanded until they seemed to fill the whole iris. But when she tried to touch the curve of his mouth, he caught her hand with his to prevent her from doing so.

"Don't start anything you're not prepared to finish," he advised her huskily.

She jerked her hand away as if the feel of his skin had scorched her fingers.

"I—I'll try not to," she whispered breathlessly.

He put her away from him and gently turned her toward the stairs. Her knees were shaking so badly, they would barely support her, and she held tightly to the banister as she climbed. When she was halfway to the top, she glanced back over her shoulder and saw that Garth was standing as she'd left him, watching her. Her hand on the rail trembled with the strength of her need for him. She longed to hold out her hand to him, to invite him to come to bed with her—to make love to her.

They remained this way, motionless figures in an immutable tableau, as time stood still. Even her heart seemed to have stopped beating.

Only Buck's impatience ended it. He had grown tired of waiting to be let out for his nightly run and when he barked, the spell was broken.

Garth moved away from the stairs to open the door for the shepherd, and Julie was free to make her way to the bedroom. Yet she was not free, and she knew that she would never be truly free again.

Chapter Ten

"Neither of you looks like you slept very much last night," Dan observed the next morning, beaming at them approvingly.

They hadn't, but not for the reason Dan obviously thought. For a long while after she'd gone to bed, Julie huddled beneath the covers and listened to Garth's steady pacing on the porch that was directly below the windows of their bedroom. Finally she heard the front door open and close as he let Buck into the house, but instead of coming inside, Garth's footsteps had echoed on the concrete of the walk. Seconds later had come the sound of a car being started. The low growl of the motor became more distant as he drove down the lane away from the house.

Because she had left the bedroom door ajar, she was able to count the hours by the chimes of the mantel clock. It was after three o'clock before Garth returned.

"Why are you still awake?" he asked when he came to bed. His voice was thick and slightly blurred.

"I was worried about you," she said. And rightly so, she thought. If one could go by his slurred speech and the sharp odor of Scotch on his breath, he was less than sober.

"Well, I'm fine," he'd said. "Go to sleep now."

He hadn't sounded fine. He'd sounded bearish and bad-tempered. And she hadn't gone to sleep. She had lain stiffly on her own side of the bed until the sky began to grow pearlescent with the approach of dawn. Though the space that separated her from Garth was not a wide one—she could easily have reached out and touched him—she had felt that there was an impenetrable barrier between them. She felt it still.

This morning Garth was so pale that his face had an almost greenish tinge, and he had no more appetite for the ham and eggs Jessie had heaped on his plate than Julie had for her own food. His usually clear eyes were red-rimmed and puffy-lidded, and from the way he narrowed them against the sunlight streaming through the kitchen windows, Julie could tell he must have a king-size headache.

From this evidence alone she would have known that Garth was suffering from a hangover; she couldn't understand how Dan and Jessie could misinterpret such symptoms and leap to the conclusion that a night of lovemaking accounted for his faintly debauched appearance. In her opinion such an over-indulgence wouldn't faze him in the least.

Julie blushed at this thought, and when she looked hurriedly away from Garth, she caught Jessie in the act of exchanging a wink with Dan.

They were just finishing breakfast when Jessie asked if they would mind going into Jackson to do some shopping for her. Garth agreed quite amiably.

He even managed a reasonable facsimile of his engaging grin.

"Why don't you two make a day of it," Jessie suggested, glancing slyly at Dan. "Do some sightseeing and have lunch in town."

Garth was noncommittal. "Maybe we will," he replied.

"I have a grocery list all made out," Jessie said as she bustled from the kitchen to collect it.

"It's cold today," Dan informed them. "They're predicting snow for tomorrow."

"I'll get our coats," Garth announced, and Julie had to admire the even tone of his voice and the easy way he strode from the room when she could imagine the effect this must have on his headache.

When he returned, he was wearing a handsome shearling car coat and carrying her heavy sweater and the fleece-lined vest as well. She knew she'd look ridiculously like a stuffed panda wearing both bulky garments but, giving herself a mental pat on the back for being so considerate of Garth's under-the-weather condition, she put them on without arguing the matter.

Jessie eyed Garth appreciatively. "I wish you'd get a jacket like that for yourself, Dan," she remarked. "Your old one is so seedy."

"What?" Dan exclaimed affrontedly. "And give up old faithful!" He shook his head sadly. "I couldn't do that, Jess. Old faithful is more than just a coat. It's kind of a good-luck charm for me."

"That's so much hooey," Jessie grumbled. "We go through this every fall, and every fall you give me the same runaround. No one is less superstitious than you are, and you know very well that coat is no lucky piece. It's only a scruffy winter parka." In an aside to Garth she explained, "It's so moth-eaten, it reminds me of an old donkey skin—and there are times when I do believe the old donkey's still wearing it!"

"But Jess," Dan countered, "if I got rid of it, I'd be so perfect you'd have nothing left to complain about." His smile was cherubic as he reasoned, "So you see, sweetheart, it's partly for your benefit that I keep it. After all, I know how dearly you love a lively difference of opinion."

They were still bickering fondly with one another when Garth and Julie let themselves out of the house to walk through the crispness of the morning air to the car. Garth winced when she allowed the door on her side to slam and eased his own shut. Before he turned the key in the ignition, he put on the sunglasses that were hooked over the visor.

Julie wanted to ask Why did you leave last night? and Where did you go? but, heeding the warning of his grim expression, she remained silent as he drove toward Jackson. Even when he stopped at a motel coffee shop on the outskirts of town, she only looked at him thoughtfully. He was paler than ever, and there was a fine film of perspiration on his forehead.

"I just want to get something for a headache," he said smoothly in answer to her unspoken question.

If Jessie hadn't asked them to do some errands for her, Julie wondered, would Garth have suffered until the headache ran its course rather than admit he had one? His face was taut with pain, and she felt genuinely sympathetic as she followed him into the café.

Garth chose a booth that was quietly situated away from the preferred tables near the windows, and when he had downed some aspirin and coffee, he sat with his head in his hands and his eyes closed. After a few minutes had passed, Julie was relieved to see that his color was markedly improved.

Because Garth had his back to the room, Julie was the first to notice the tall, strikingly attractive girl who was purposefully making her way through the coffee shop in their direction. From under a broad-brimmed leather hat that was trimmed with feathers, her luxuriant mane of taffy-colored hair fell straight and smooth to her athletic young shoulders and she wore the tourist's standard uniform—fringed suede jacket, western-style shirt, tight blue jeans, and hand-tooled boots—with a panache that belied her ingenuous appearance. And although her clothing was unisex, her well-endowed figure was unmistakably female.

"Hello again," she caroled as she sat next to Garth in the booth. After a single dismissing look at Julie, her cornflower-blue eyes laughed into his. "I see you found your way home safely last night."

Garth smiled and said, "Hello, er—"

"Mindy. Mindy Stryker," the girl provided, affecting a pretty pout that called attention to her full mouth as it expressed her disappointment that he'd forgotten her name.

"Mindy," Garth repeated. He was still smiling at her, and it was obvious that he was intrigued by her alluring manner. "This is Julie—"

"Nice to meet you," Mindy interrupted uninterestedly, without shifting her avid gaze from Garth's face.

Julie glanced from Mindy to Garth. She studied him with renewed interest and decided, uncomfortably, that his vaguely ravaged, tortured look of this

127

morning suited him every bit as well as his smile did. In fact, she told herself disgustedly, he looked very much the Byronic hero—romantically brooding and intensely mysterious.

"I'm so glad I ran into you again," Mindy purred. "Daddy wants to leave for home today, and since we're practically neighbors, I thought you'd like to have my address in San Francisco."

Julie was fascinated by Mindy's demonstration of self-confidence and watched every move as the younger girl rummaged through her shoulder bag and removed a thin tube of lip liner. She pulled a paper napkin from the dispenser at the center of the table and scribbled carelessly on it with the strawberry-colored cosmetic.

"We skeptical Scorpios have to stick together," she commented pertly as she folded the napkin to keep the lipstick from smearing and slipped it into the breast pocket of Garth's shirt. Her fingers toyed with the fleecy lining of his coat. "Besides," she cooed, her voice throaty and brazenly intimate, "you're the only *good* thing that's happened to me on this whole ghastly trip. Until last night it was a deadly bore. You really knocked me out with your impression of Neil Diamond. The Cowboy Bar will never be the same—and neither will I!"

From beneath the fan of her lashes Mindy flirted with Garth, turning the full force of her extraordinary eyes on him for a full minute before she glanced over her shoulder at the distinguished middle-aged man who was waiting for her by the door. Her pout became more pronounced.

"Daddy's getting impatient to leave," she said petulantly. "I really *do* hope you'll call me the next time you're going to be in San Francisco, Garth." As she sauntered toward the exit she waved a slender hand with practiced flamboyance and called, "Ciao, darling."

When the door of the café had closed behind the Strykers, Julie slid out of the booth. She batted her eyelashes at Garth before she stalked angrily away from him.

"Ciao, darling!" she said, in a fair reproduction of Mindy's dulcet delivery.

Garth threw some money on the table and caught up with her just as she reached the car. She maintained a fuming silence while he walked around the sedan to get in on the driver's side, but as soon as he sat behind the wheel she attacked waspishly.

"Thanks for at least remembering my name. When I think of how concerned I was when you drove off last night, I could just . . . just—"

"Throw another tantrum?" Garth prompted imperturbably.

"I thought you were drowning your sorrows," she rushed on irately, "and instead you were kicking up your heels!"

"The one doesn't necessarily preclude the other," he retorted, "but that's beside the point. I don't suppose it ever entered your mind that I might have been working up the courage to give you an honest answer to your question."

"My question?"

"As to why I don't parade my feelings for all the world to see."

"You needed courage for that? Ha!" she scoffed shrilly and was pleased to see him wince this time. "I've combed the hayseeds out of my hair and I don't believe that line any more than I believe that mock turtle soup is made with mock turtles."

"I don't give a damn what you believe," Garth cut in. "It's the truth nevertheless. And since I've never before welshed on a bargain, I intend to try to explain it to you. Whether you listen or not is up to you."

His menacing expression muzzled her as effectively as the low value he placed on her opinion of him. Julie swallowed hard, attempting to dislodge the choking lump of shame in her throat. She recognized that she'd been ranting like a fishwife and she felt diminished by it.

"I—I'll listen," she stammered.

Garth removed the sunglasses and rubbed his eyes with the heels of his hands before replacing them. "It can be summed up with the adage 'old habits die hard,' " he said.

"But how . . ." She hesitated.

"How did it get to be a habit?" he finished evenly. "To understand that, you'd have to know what my parents were like." Before he continued, he rolled the seat into a half reclining position and slouched into it, with one knee jackknifed and propped against the steering wheel and his head resting on the seat back. He closed his eyes, and his face became an expressionless mask.

"My mother's father was a silent partner in Falconer's. From the time she was in her cradle, both of my grandfathers hoped for her marriage to Dad. It was actually more of a business merger than a marriage," he said steadily, "and once they'd produced me, there was no physical side to their relationship.

"Since the business was of little importance to Mother, the time was bound to come when she realized how dissatisfied she was with her quasimarriage. After her father died and I'd reached school age, she had a lot of time on her hands, and to fill it she enrolled in an art course at our local college. She fell in love with her professor—or according to Dad, she *thought* she did. She was very discreet, very careful to preserve the appearance that she and Dad were the perfect couple, so that was all right, but the man was much younger. To my father, that was a greater offense than the fact that she'd become involved in an affair."

Garth sighed deeply. "Mother asked Dad for a divorce but he turned her down, and for several years she went along with him. Occasionally she'd bring up the possibility of divorce, but he refused to even discuss it with her. It just wasn't done in either of their families, and I suppose initially that carried as much weight with her as anything. She hadn't much natural inclination to go against precedent. It was later, when she started to get desperate, that Dad played his trump card: He told Mother she was free to leave whenever she wanted to, but if she did, she could forget she'd ever had a son."

His mouth tightened ruefully. "Dad and Mother were very much of the old school. Displays of emotion were regarded as suspiciously tacky. Like most of their crowd, they'd rather have been accused of being an axe-murderer than be guilty of nouveau riche behavior, so through all of this they never once raised their voices to each other. The whole thing was conducted so politely, they might have been discussing the weather or something equally impersonal."

He opened his eyes and smiled wryly as he admitted, "The way I sound just now." He sat up and fished the keys out of his pocket.

"What finally happened between your mother and the young man she fell in love with?" Julie asked huskily.

"He got fed up with waiting for her and left the area. He didn't let her know he was going away, much less say good-bye, and even when Mother learned he'd gone back East, she took the news without turning a hair—except in the privacy of her own bedroom. Afterward she drifted aimlessly from one affair to another but she never fell in love again."

His mouth thinned to a hard line. "A few years later, when she heard that her former lover had gotten married, she attempted suicide. Dad was so shocked that she'd go to such a barbaric extreme that he agreed to a legal separation."

Although he started the car with an abrupt, angry jab, his voice was controlled to the point of gentleness. "Mother lives in Arizona now. She dabbles in ceramics and painting and now and then she 'discovers' a new protégé—always male, always young and good-looking—in short, always a stud. She seems fairly content, so I guess it was better late than never."

Julie shook her head in confusion. "I still don't understand your reluctance to tell me this last night."

Despite the concealing lenses of his sunglasses, the impact of Garth's cynicism struck her like a blow. His scrutiny of her was ruthless and openly disbelieving.

"There's an envelope in the console," he said. His

132

tone was barbed. "You might find its contents enlightening."

She retrieved the envelope and was immediately overcome by an inexplicable feeling of apprehension. She held it without opening it for a few moments, at a loss as to why the mere idea of looking inside should fill her with such dread. The sour taste of fear dried her mouth, and in an effort to reason away her anxiety she examined the envelope as if it were vital that she memorize the smallest detail of its manufacture.

It was letter-size and made of plain brown paper, with metal prongs to seal the flap. The folds along the sides were partially torn and it was dog-eared, but apart from its somewhat battered condition there was nothing to distinguish it from countless millions of others.

Given all this preparation, it came as an anti-climax when she opened the flap and removed the thin sheaf of newspaper clippings the envelope contained. She leafed through them quickly and saw that they offered an account of the bribery scandal, her parents' deaths, and the clearing of her father's name.

More confused than before, she slid the articles back inside the envelope and methodically sealed it. Her eyes were dark and troubled when she looked up at Garth. Only then did she become aware that they had arrived at the supermarket and that he had been studying her reaction.

A smile softened the deeply indented corners of his mouth and he lifted a silky strand of hair away from her cheek to tuck it behind her ear.

"You really don't recognize any of it, do you," he observed gently.

Again Julie shook her head. "I'm sorry. I realize that I *should,* but I don't."

"I found the clippings in your suitcase along with your note after you left. They came as quite a shock since you'd always seemed to be so uninformed about your parents." He cupped her cheek with his hand and any desire she might have had to turn away evaporated.

"When you disappeared," he said in a low tone, "Charlotte suggested that the clippings established the motive for what you'd done. She theorized that it was all premeditated—that you'd married me in order to exact some kind of revenge for the slander your father had suffered."

Julie's eyes widened incredulously. "And you believed her?" she breathed.

"I didn't know *what* to believe," Garth replied honestly, "but it's another reason I was so ready to be convinced that you were in love with Dan." His fingertips moved slowly over her face, warmly caressing the delicate line of her cheek and exploring the little hollow just beneath her jaw. "I guess I didn't want to think that you could be so vindictive."

"Have you thought all this time that I've been faking not being able to remember?"

"I haven't been sure—not about that or anything else where you're concerned." His mouth compressed, and he withdrew his hand from her face. "Then last night . . ." He shrugged. "For a while, I wondered whether you were trying to start the whole thing all over again."

Deprived of his touch, Julie felt lonely and cold.

She shivered and stared through the windshield at the towering, slate-blue spire of Mt. Wilson. Its stark outline danced and shimmered through the mist of tears in her eyes.

"I used to—" She faltered into a stunned silence.

"What, Julie?" Garth tersely demanded.

She cleared her throat and made another attempt. "There's an aerial tramway that goes to the top of Mount Wilson," she said haltingly. "I used to like to ride it to the summit when I had some problem I needed to work out. The view is . . . magnificent. It's like the whole world is spread out before you, never changing, yet never the same. And it's so still . . . so infinite . . . even the biggest worries seem small. It used to help me to keep things in perspective."

"You're beginning to remember more about the past each day, aren't you, Julie?" Garth said quietly.

"Yes," she whispered shakily. "And—oh, Garth —I'm not sure I want to."

When she blindly reached out for him, his arms encircled her and gathered her protectively close to the strong bulwark of his chest.

"I'm so afraid," she cried. Her hands clutched almost violently at his shoulders. "Hold me, Garth. Please hold me."

Chapter Eleven

They drove to Jenny Lake Lodge for lunch and returned to Dan's house in midafternoon to find Dan was in high good humor, using only a cane for support as he hobbled around the yard. He promptly enlisted Garth's assistance in the chore of splitting and stacking a supply of firewood for the winter and they went off to one of the outbuildings together.

"Can I help with anything?" Julie asked Jessie.

"Not just now," Jessie replied as she stored the last of the groceries they'd brought from town. "Why don't you go have a nap? You look a bit weary."

"Maybe I will," Julie gratefully agreed.

First she had a long, relaxing bath. After hastily shedding her clothes, she pinned her hair loosely on top of her head and added perfumed bath salts to the water liberally. She eased into the steaming water and soaked until it became tepid, almost dozing off in the tub. She barely managed to wrap a fluffy towel around herself and crawl under the blankets before she fell asleep.

It was early evening when she awoke. She stretched luxuriously, feeling truly refreshed, and realized that she was not alone in the room.

"Garth?" she whispered. She could just make out

the darker shadow of his head and shoulders framed by the night sky in the window.

He came to the nightstand on the far side of the bed and switched on the lamp. She smiled drowsily up at him and saw that he had recently showered and changed. His hair was slicked down, damp and glossy, and he was wearing finely tailored gray slacks with a darker gray sweater. He sat on the edge of the bed and smiled at her. His eyes were a clear green-gold and he seemed to radiate vitality.

"You look much better after your rest," he observed.

"You look better too," she murmured. "Woodcutting must agree with you."

"It's amazingly good medicine for a hangover," he said dryly. "In fact it's good medicine for whatever ails a man, body or soul, but it's tough on the unsuspecting hide!"

He chuckled and held out one hand, palm up, to reveal the bandages covering the base of his fingers. Julie exclaimed sympathetically and, leaning on one elbow, pulled herself partly upright to look at his injured palm. She lay a fingertip lightly on one of the smaller blisters that he'd left unbandaged.

"It must be terribly painful." She wished she could dare to kiss the injuries.

"It's not too bad," he drawled.

She heard the levity in his voice and cautiously raised her eyes to his.

"Of course," he reconsidered thoughtfully, "it might be too much for an ordinary man to take, but I think I can stand it."

Somehow she kept a straight face. "You must have split a lot of firewood," she said admiringly.

"Let's put it this way," he qualified, pretending to be morose, "if Dan and Jessie don't keep warm this winter, it won't be my fault."

She laughed. "I think Dan's flair for melodrama is catching. Some of it seems to have rubbed off on you."

"Thank you." Garth solemnly inclined his head. "I take that as a compliment."

"It was intended as one!"

"In their way, Dan and Jessie are two of the finest people I've ever known. And they certainly complement each other."

Julie nodded gravely.

"I might return the flattery," Garth said. "There's at least one thing you and Jessie have in common."

"What's that?" she asked breathlessly.

"Neither of you gives the impression of being overly concerned with being fashionably dressed."

His eyes wandered lazily downward over the flawless skin of her shoulders to settle on the full curves of her breasts, calling to her attention how much of her was left exposed by the precariously anchored towel. She colored to the roots of her hair and tried unobtrusively to hitch it up a bit.

"In Jessie's case, such an attitude is understandable," he mused. "She has a body most women in their twenties would give ten years off their lives to possess, so clothes to her are like gilt to the lily."

"Do you especially admire full-figured women?" Julie asked, hoping he would give a negative reply.

He nodded with daunting enthusiasm. "What man wouldn't admire a woman with a figure like Jessie's? She's a veritable goddess. I'd like to have seen her when she was young. She really must have been something."

Julie's expression was crestfallen and she hurriedly lowered her eyes.

"*However,*" Garth asserted, "it's always been my contention that there are more important considerations than size." He ran one finger along the slope of her collarbone and continued audaciously, barely suppressing his laughter. "If a woman has the right instincts and she's a good armful and her, uh, measurements provide a nice *handful,* I've never been known to complain."

Julie's eyes flashed up at him. Her cheeks were vivid with embarrassment. "Did you wake me up just so you'd have someone to tease?"

"No," he denied evenly. "It's not that you aren't delightfully easy to provoke, but my primary mission was to let you know that Dan and Jessie have gone out for the evening and"—he paused briefly for emphasis—"in their absence, *I* have prepared dinner." He stood and walked toward the door. "It's on the table and if you don't hurry, it'll be cold before we have a chance to eat it, so I'll see you downstairs in a few minutes, okay?"

"Okay," she echoed faintly, taken aback by the idea of Garth slaving over a hot stove.

He nodded and went into the hall, only to lean back around the edge of the door and deliver a villainous ogle.

"Do me a favor," he said. "Wear your dress for dinner."

"If you l-like," she acceded diffidently.

"Oh, I like." He grinned meaningfully. "I like very much!"

After he had gone, she threw back the covers and hurried to get into her clothes. Her hands were made all thumbs by her excitement and she ruined two pairs of pantyhose before she gave up and slipped her sandals on over her bare feet. As she brushed her hair until it shone richly dark in contrast to her fair skin, she surveyed her appearance in the mirror.

The dress had a halter top and a simple, knife-pleated skirt. Its warm coral, gold, and pink hues suited her very well. She applied a little eye shadow and some peach-tinted lip gloss and she was ready. At the top of the stairs she stopped to catch her breath before she made a sedate descent.

Garth was waiting in the hall just outside of the kitchen. He was playing the role of maitre d' to the hilt and, without speaking, he led her to the table, where he seated her with a great show of formality. He filled her wineglass with Cold Duck and removed the warming cover from the plate at her place with a flourish. When she saw the submarine sandwich, the pickle, and potato salad that were arranged there, she burst into laughter.

Between giggles she asked weakly, "H-how can a s-sandwich and salad get cold?"

"It's pastrami," Garth revealed, pleased by how well his audience had received his joke.

"Mmmm, my favorite!" Julie said enthusiastically as she bit hungrily into hers.

"I remember," Garth said.

He offered her some corn chips and took a handful for himself. He seemed not to have noticed that she'd startled herself when she'd dredged up another memory, even if it was only about pastrami.

"Where did Dan and Jessie go?"

Garth grinned widely. "Would you believe a square dance?"

"With Dan's gout? That doesn't seem very likely."

"Exactly my reaction," Garth confirmed sagely, "but that's where they claimed they were headed. They particularly stressed the point that they wouldn't be home before we'd gone to bed."

"They'll probably skulk around outside until they see the lights go out."

"In that case, maybe we should make sure we have an early night."

His voice was suddenly serious, and Julie's heart skipped a beat before it knocked heavily against her ribs. She sought to hide the fact that he'd disconcerted her by taking a sip of wine, only to sputter when it went down the wrong way.

Except for this lapse, however, their meal was a pleasant one. They conversed easily and as they lingered at the table, he drinking coffee and she her preferred tea, it was the Cold Duck that launched Garth on the topic of how they'd met.

"This is the winery you used to work for." He indicated the label on the bottle. "Their Cold Duck isn't bad, but they have an exceptional Pinot Noir and a fine Gamay Beaujolais. Their reputation is based on the excellence of their varietal wines."

"How did we happen to meet again after all those years?" she asked.

"We were introduced by friends." His eyes glinted with devilish enjoyment, and he immediately contradicted his statement. "No. That's not the precise truth," he said. "That was how we met for the *third* time."

"Now you've aroused my curiosity!"

Garth chuckled. "I told you that you'd worked as a tour guide."

Julie nodded eagerly.

"Well, a friend of mine, Rod Parent, was dating another of the tour guides. Things were progressing satisfactorily between them until you came on the scene."

"How did I interfere?"

"You were assigned to share Betty's cottage," he replied, smiling nostalgically. "Rod asked me to agree to a blind date with you in order to get you out of their hair, so he and Betty could have the place to themselves for the night. I didn't place your name until later and I wasn't too keen on the prospect. I hadn't been on a blind date since Lord knows when, but I owed Rod a favor, so I caved in. Needless to say, since I was roped into it, my mood wasn't the best, and that's why I gave you such a hard time."

"A hard time. . . ." she repeated blankly.

"Rod and I arrived about four in the afternoon. It was Betty's day off, and they were getting an early start, so I had some time to kill. I decided to spend part of it going through the winery. They hadn't told me you were the guide on duty, and I was disruptive." He shook his head. "Perhaps I'm being too easy on myself, because you'd only just finished your training, and it was obvious you were nervous. At the time though, I was feeling so perverse, it seemed entertaining to heckle you."

Julie's eyes were round with disbelief. "That was an awful thing to do!"

"I know," Garth conceded, shrugging and trying unsuccessfully to look contrite. "But, never fear, you got your own back on me! Besides, you blushed so

142

predictably. I'd never seen a girl as easy to embarrass as you. I kept interrupting you and every time I did, you had to go back to the start of your spiel. Apparently that was the only way you could recite it."

She laughed merrily with him. "It sounds funny enough now," she commented when she had sobered, "but I'll bet I wasn't at all amused at the time."

"No, you weren't," Garth said wryly, "and I have to admit that was a major part of the attraction for me. I was taking out my resentment on you. It wasn't a very nice thing to do, but I wasn't in a 'nice' frame of mind."

"You said I got even with you though," she reminded him.

"And then some," Garth exclaimed. "The last stop on the tour was the gift shop and tasting room. By then I was feeling fairly well pleased with myself. Actually, *smug* is what I was. You were passing out wine to the people on the tour and you served the other customers and opened a fresh bottle before you asked if I'd care for a sample. You were so damnably demure that I thought, This girl can't be for real! I couldn't resist making one last wisecrack—and frankly it was a more than usually explicit one—at which point you poured a whole fifth of Chablis right where it did the most to dampen my spirits."

"Is that all?" She feigned nonchalance. She was finding it hard to keep from laughing.

"What do you mean, 'Is that *all*'? It was cold as hell!" He shuddered at the recollection and gave her a pained look. "My God, woman, what more do you want?"

"I'd like to know what you said to prompt such a reaction."

Garth looked pointedly at the teacup she had just refilled. "I don't think I care to risk repeating it while you're holding a *hot* drink."

"I'll put it down then."

She did this and watched him so expectantly that he shifted uneasily in his chair.

"I'm not sure I can quote myself exactly," he stalled.

"A general idea will do," she persisted brightly. She leaned one elbow on the table and cupped her chin with her hand to cover a furtive smile. If she didn't know better, she'd think Garth was blushing. The tips of his ears were certainly a healthy pink.

"Well—" He hesitated. "Look, Julie, it's going to sound really stupid under these conditions."

"I don't mind," she said airily.

"Of course *you* don't! I'm the one who's going to look like an ass." He slammed his own cup down on the table and sighed resignedly. "All right," he growled, "since you're so blasted anxious to hear it. It was something to the effect that I wouldn't be content with just a sample, and that the real test of manhood was being able to, uh, make love—for as long as it takes to empty an entire bottle of wine—"

"Only you meant emptying the bottle by drinking the wine," she finished sweetly.

Garth nodded. He was decidedly flustered. "And you proceeded to pour it out in two seconds or less!" A foolish grin spread across his face. "And to add insult to injury you apologized for revealing my *shortcomings*. So I figure I got more than I deserved."

"Altogether, it doesn't sound as if it was a very

promising start to a blind date," Julie remarked pensively.

"It wasn't. And the evening was more of the same. If anything it was *worse*. You were steamed because I might have gotten you fired. Still, you had to acknowledge I'd gone to bat for you with your boss. So when I explained the problem Rod and Betty were having finding some privacy, you insisted on being dropped off in town. You planned to go to a double feature and stay at the movie theater until it was late enough to go home.

"I told myself I was happy to be rid of you. I thought I never wanted to see you again. But I couldn't get you out of my mind. The next weekend I went back to the winery with Rod—he was my excuse, you see—and that was when I discovered who your father was."

"Did that time go any better?"

His smile faded. "Not much," he said glumly. "I made the fatal mistake of kissing you. From then on I was sunk and I knew it."

"Didn't we have any common interests?" she asked wistfully.

"Enough, I suppose," he replied brusquely. "We both enjoyed all sorts of music, wind-surfing, going to the beach—that type of thing."

She could tell from the abstracted way he'd answered that he was deep in thought and, sighing regretfully over the fact that their lighthearted conversation had ended on such a low note, she began clearing the table.

They did go to bed early that night but because of

her nap Julie was wakeful. She lay quietly with her back to Garth, reliving the events of the evening.

After they'd tidied the kitchen and set out some food for Buck, Garth put a Brahms concerto on the stereo. They hadn't bothered to light the fire, since neither of them wanted to leave it burning when they turned in. When they put Buck outside, they waited on the porch for him to complete his nightly circuit of the grounds and they'd laughed at his antics as he frolicked around the yard, as frisky as a puppy, until he ran out of sight behind the garage.

Garth stood by the railing with his feet planted firmly apart and his head thrown back as he looked up at the sky. In this lordly stance his pride was flagrantly apparent, but for some reason Julie was no longer put off by it.

"Will you look at those stars," Garth said in a subdued voice. "They're so close, you'd swear you could reach up and grab a handful of them."

"I know," she agreed reverently. "It's so clear, it's hard to believe that snow is forecast for tomorrow."

It was true that there wasn't a cloud in the sky, but the night air was icy; a penetrating wind was blowing from the northwest. Julie snuggled more closely into her sweater, burying her chin in the heavy shawl collar. There was no moon and although the more prominent glaciers and snowfields dimly reflected the starlight, the saw-toothed ridges of the Tetons were more envisioned than actually seen.

The howl of a coyote reverberated from far away and the darkness underscored the eeriness of the cry. Julie felt the short hairs at the nape of her neck stand on end; the skin on her forearms broke out in goose-flesh. The call was repeated, and from a different direction the counterpoint was picked up when another animal joined the plaintive song. She sidled closer to Garth while they listened to the desolate duet. On and on went the weird harmony, and the wild cries of yearning spoke to something equally primitive within her.

Garth was also affected. His shoulders were hunched and his hands were clenched about the porchrail so tightly, the knuckles were a stark bone-white through his sun-browned skin.

"God," he muttered hoarsely. "That's got to be the loneliest sound in the world."

Wanting to comfort him, Julie had put her hand over one of his, but he hadn't seemed to notice.

Would she ever truly understand him? she wondered. Somehow she didn't think so. She knew some of his moods; she had learned—the hard way—that the color of his eyes was a reliable indicator of a few of them: Gray for anger, for disapproval, for pride. Green for contentment, for concern—for passion? Gold for humor, for teasing, for happiness. And sometimes they were a mixture of all three. What did that signify? Doubt, perhaps? Or rare indecision?

It bewildered her to think that for the past few days he had so frequently questioned her reasons for marrying him, while she had never once mustered sufficient courage to ask him why he had married her. For her it was enough to know that Garth was her husband and that she loved him. *Oh, God,* she acknowledged silently, *I love him so much.* Everything else seemed to pale into insignificance in the radiance of that miracle.

What was he thinking? He was lying on his back with his arms folded behind his head and although he was perfectly still, she knew he was still awake. He was so near, she was enveloped by the heat from his body, but he seemed so far away.

I wish—She closed her eyes tightly, concentrating with every particle of her being on her unspoken prayer. *I wish he'd kiss me. I want him to touch me. I wish he'd speak to me, say my name.* Only *my name. If he says my name before I can count to one hundred,* she promised herself, *everything will be all right.*

Willing him to give her this small omen, she began counting slowly, and when she reached fifty, even more slowly. By the time she reached sixty, she knew she couldn't bear his silence any longer.

Almost inaudibly she asked, "Garth, are you awake?"

"Um-hmmm." He sounded sleepy but the suspension of his regular respirations, the sudden tensing of his muscles had given away how alert he really was.

"How much longer will we be staying here?"

"I don't know, Julie." He sighed wearily. "A few days maybe."

His tone of voice discouraged further conversation, and although she wanted to squirm uncomfortably, for a while she lay quietly. The silence between them became more and more oppressive. She was being suffocated by it and she wanted to scream.

"Garth," she murmured, and quickly, before she could lose her nerve, she requested, "would you tell me more about our courtship."

"For God's sake, Julie—"

"Please," she implored him fervently.

It was some moments before he replied, and when he did, there was an oddly strangled quality about his voice, as if he were having trouble breathing properly.

"What would you like to know?" he asked.

"Did we kiss a lot?"

"That's about all we did do at first."

"Why only at first?"

"You wouldn't let me make love to you until we were married, and it got to be more than I could take, constantly trying to turn off in the middle of things. So I stopped kissing you."

"What did we do when we weren't kissing?"

"We had a lot of rather heated debates—arguments— Hell!" he said disgustedly. "The truth of the matter is, we fought!"

"What did we fight about?"

"Everything. Nothing. Who knows?" The mattress dipped a bit as he turned his head to look at her, but other than that he didn't change position. "I think we used to fight because we were so frustrated. I wanted to make love to you, and you wanted it too. . . . At least part of you did. I think you were fighting with yourself more than with me. And we never really talked. I've gotten to know you better in the last few days than in all the weeks we were dating."

The pall of silence descended again while Julie mulled this over. Finally she turned onto her other side and lay facing him.

"Garth," she called his name softly.

"Hmmm?"

"Would you kiss me now?"

This time he was quiet for so long that sh
to fear he might have fallen asleep. She
breath while she waited for his answer, s

that, when at last he spoke, she started.

"Dammit, Julie!" he snapped. "I'm not made of stone. If I kiss you now, I won't stop."

Driven by her longing to be close to him, she moved compulsively nearer. Her body was aching with the need for him. "I won't want you to stop," she whispered.

Garth remained warily motionless. "How can you be so certain of that?"

"I don't know. I just feel it."

"God help me if I'm wrong," he groaned, "but I feel it too."

Before the sound of his voice had completely died away, Garth had turned onto his side and his arm was hard around her, pulling her close to the taut length of his body. His lips were trailing over her face, leaving fiery little kisses on her forehead, her temples, her cheeks, while her own lips were relishing the raspiness of stubble, the clean yet faintly salty taste of his jaw, his throat, his chin—planting exploratory kisses on whichever part of him happened to be within her reach.

She was gasping his name, sobbing without tears, tormented by an unbearable craving for the touch of his lips and when his mouth intercepted hers, she returned the hungry pressure of his lips with undisguised eagerness, meeting the intoxicating feint and parry of his tongue with an almost desperate eroticism. Her arms held him fiercely; her hands were slippery with perspiration as they caressed the smooth hard skin at the small of his back. She felt feverishly restless, and her body arched with unwitting provocation in response to the least movement his.

"Slowly, Julie. Slowly, darling," he crooned against her lips. Through half-closed eyelids she watched dazedly as he raised his head. In spite of the darkness of the bedroom, she seemed to be viewing him through a roseate haze as he smiled down at her.

"We have all the time in the world. We have all the rest of our lives." His mouth descended to nuzzle her ear, and a tremor of excitement shook her when he caught the fleshy part of the lobe between the sharp edges of his teeth to nibble it gently and murmur one last pledge: "We have as long as it takes to drink the wine."

He had unbuttoned the pajama top and pushed it away from her shoulders and now he slid one arm underneath her, effortlessly lifting her in order to remove the jacket completely, and as he did so, the thrust of his unclad body against hers was incredibly exciting. His hands were roughened from working with the wood and his fingertips had a slight grittiness that was electrifying as he softly fondled her breasts. Her nipples tingled and grew proudly erect in the warm bowl of his palms.

Again and again he kissed her, teasing her with the exquisite thoroughness of his lovemaking, for there was no part of her that escaped his attention. She reached a state of frenzied awareness when he sought the pleasure points of her body and she felt the tip of his tongue—now probing the honied recesses of her mouth, now moistly tracing the convolutions of her ear, now burning hotly across her shoulders, now circling and invading the tiny hollow of her navel, now brushing sweet feathery patterns on her breasts.

She wove her fingers through his hair to cradle his head, gently at first and then with fast-rising urgency

151

as she reveled in the sensuous contact of his lips. Blissfully freed of restraint, her hands wandered over his body with abandon, learning the sleek texture of his skin, loving the potent rippling of superbly conditioned muscle, marveling that he should be capable of such strength and at the same time such tenderness.

She was totally pliant and her body instinctively conformed to the contours of his as he molded her to him more intimately. Her arms and legs were all silky smoothness while his were hair-roughened. Her body was delicately rounded where his was ruggedly angular; all womanly softness where his was hard and masculine. His hands continued their tantalizing explorations, stroking over the length of her spine, pausing to savor the graceful curve from waist to hip, lingering on the velvety flesh of her thighs.

Her delight was so overwhelming that she was frightened by its intensity, but her alarm was instantly communicated to him, and he claimed her mouth yet again, conquering her fear with the immediacy of his passion. He eased her onto her back, following her with the demanding weight of his body, and for a time the hard unrelenting pressure he exerted caused her pain that drowned out awareness of anything else. Her eyes opened wide with surprise, but as quickly as it had begun, the pain was gone. For only a moment longer they were two separate entities, and in the next instant the final fragile barrier was sundered, and they were one.

Julie had thought her pleasure could not possibly increase any further, but now she was journeying through a strange and secret world of sensuality with

Garth as her guide. Knowing she would be forever lost without him, she clung to him without reservation as his wild caresses generated a new and delicious tension within her.

Please, please—oh, please! Her lips moved soundlessly to form the supplication, though she knew not for what she was pleading.

She was adrift in a tumultuous sea of desire, melting and floating away from herself, losing the essence of herself in Garth's sure possession of her. And when at last his ardor transported her to the very crest of the tidal wave, she had become pure sensation; she found that she had been recreated by the ecstasy they shared. Her odyssey with Garth cast her up on a pagan shore whose beauty was limited only by the boundless depths of her love for him, and she cried out breathlessly, "I love you!"

"Beautiful," he murmured raggedly. "So beautiful."

Garth's breathing was erratic. His lips ranged freely over her face, and his hands quieted her body. They continued to hold one another while their pulses slowed and a gentle feeling of languor seeped in to replace passion.

When Garth finally moved away from her in order to arrange the blankets around them, he kept one arm around her so that she lay snugly against his side with her head on his shoulder. Her face was tucked into the warm curve of his neck, and with every breath she drew, she inhaled the heady, musky scent of his skin. His free hand was rhythmically smoothing the damp tendrils of hair away from her face, and her limbs grew leaden with relaxation. Beneath the palm of the hand that rested on his chest, she could feel the crispness of hair, the heat of his body, the steady thud of his heart.

"Sleep now, my darling," he whispered drowsily.

"Yes," she agreed with a sigh. And completely contented, utterly fulfilled, she did.

Chapter Twelve

Julie was having the loveliest dream. Garth was embracing her, and his hands were moving over her; tenderly gliding over the silken plains, enfolding the warm contours of the hills and searching out the secret valleys.

"Wake up, sleepyhead," urged a deep voice close to her ear.

Not wanting to relinquish her fantasy, she murmured a protest and tried to recapture sleep.

"Wake up, Julie," the voice repeated, and this time she recognized it as Garth's.

He touched his lips to her shoulder; his hands grew more persuasive, and she realized she wasn't dreaming at all. Memories of the joys he'd shown her in the night bubbled to the surface of her mind, and she opened her eyes. In the dim predawn light she had to strain to see his face close to hers on the pillow.

"Good morning, wife." He was smiling and his features were relaxed and smoothed of worry.

Shyly returning his smile, she asked, "Is it morning? It's still so dark."

"It's cloudy. In fact it's snowing."

She stifled a yawn. "Even so, it must be awfully early. What time is it?"

"Why all the interest in time? Are you in a hurry to go somewhere?"

"No, just curious."

Garth stretched his arm out from under the covers to check his watch, and the movement admitted a draft of cold air. He had to bring his wrist close to his eyes before he was able to make out the face of the watch, and in the process her nose was pressed against him. The mat of dark curling hair on his chest tickled maddeningly, making her want to sneeze before his hold on her loosened and his arm snaked back into the warmth beneath the blankets.

"It's almost seven o'clock," he declared.

Craning her neck to kiss him on the chin, she inquired lightly, "Almost?"

"Well," he replied slowly, "actually, it's only six fifteen."

"What are you doing awake so early?"

"I'd have thought the answer to that was obvious," he teased.

His hands had resumed their wandering, and when he briefly crushed her to him, she became aware of his arousal. Her face flamed, and he laughed deep in his throat, amused by her confusion.

"Ask a silly question . . ." he chided.

"But you didn't give me a silly answer!" she objected breathlessly. His excitement had ignited her own, and already her desire was quickening and flowering beneath his skillful touch.

"No?" he queried. He raised an eyebrow at her, shamming disbelief. He was acutely conscious of the burgeoning response of her body.

"No," she affirmed.

She caught her lower lip between her teeth to keep from crying out her pleasure as his thumb stroked over the sensitive tip of a nipple. Her hands had crept up his chest to his shoulders and now she wound her arms around his neck. She was trembling, and her eyes were alight with passion as she pulled his head down and lifted her mouth to his. They kissed lovingly, lingeringly, but with a certain sweet restraint; each of them purposely forestalling the final rapture in order to savor it all the more. And when the kiss had ended, Garth buried his face in her hair.

"Have you any idea how much I've wanted to wake up in the morning and find you in my arms?" he asked roughly. "How I've wanted to see your hair spread out on the pillow beside me? I'd like to wrap myself in it. I'd like to wrap *you* in it—see you wear it like a satin cape."

As he spoke he twined a shining skein of her hair around his fingers and let it fall across her face. He repeated this ritual with another strand and another, running his fingers through her hair to loosen it and fan it out until a fine veil of it covered her face. No sooner had he finished arranging it when he parted it to kiss her through the gauzy curtain, and for a long entrancing interlude the silence in the room was disturbed only by whispered words and muted cries of love.

When Julie awoke for the second time that morning, the chinook had set in from the southwest and the sky was a clear, windswept blue. Already the temperature had moderated and the snow was melting. A cadential drumming sound marked the rapid

157

thaw as the runoff from the roof of the house over-
flowed the gutters and dripped from the eaves. Shafts
of sunshine were deflected by the remaining snow
and poured with blinding intensity through the windows to gather in shimmering pools of light on the
walls and ceiling of the bedroom.

She opened her eyes slowly and saw that Garth
was still beside her. He was lying with his head
braced by one hand and it was apparent that he had
been watching her. It made her feel peculiarly de-
fenseless to think of him studying her while she slept.

As if he'd read her thoughts he smiled, as brilliant-
ly as the light in the room, as warmly as the balmy
breeze. He bent over her and brushed the off-center
dimple in her chin with his lips.

"I've been wondering how you happened to come
by that scar," he explained softly. "Did you injure
yourself in one of your childhood adventures?"

Julie's smile froze, half formed. Her breath caught
in her throat when she corrected him, "It's not a
scar, it's a cleft!" Her sleep-husky voice was edged
with surprising vehemence, and its harshness startled her. She inhaled deeply, trying to regain her
composure before she ventured uncertainly, "Or
maybe it's some kind of birthmark. But so far as I
know, I've always had it."

"No, Julie." Garth shook his head. "You didn't
have it when you were a little girl."

He ran the edge of his thumb along it and as he
traced it she could visualize the tiny crescentic inden-
tation. His brows were drawn together as he puzzled
over it.

"I asked you about it once before and you changed
the subject. You were uneasy then too. It's nothing

to be self-conscious about, you know," he reassured her. "It adds character to your face and, if anything, it's endearing."

"I'm not uneasy, dammit!" She jerked her chin away from his touch. "And I'm not self-conscious about it because *it isn't a scar*!"

Calmly Garth tried to reason with her. "If you'd look at it closely—"

"Please," she moaned. She hid the mark from him with her hand. A fine tremor started at the tips of her fingers and quickly became less localized until she was shaking all over. "Please! Can't you just forget it?"

Garth was baffled by Julie's reaction. One minute she had been unnecessarily agitated and the next she had gone absolutely inert. Thinking to comfort her, he raised his hand to smooth the tumbled cloud of hair back from her forehead but when Julie caught sight of a blur of motion from the corner of her eye, she flinched and reflexively threw her arm in front of her face as though she were warding off a blow. Her eyes were wide and glazed, and she stared up at him fixedly before she rolled away from him and simultaneously curled her body into a tight knot of misery.

Garth was stunned. "My God, Julie!" he exclaimed crossly. "You're behaving as if I'd made a habit of beating you. After last night, don't you know I would never intentionally do anything to harm you? What's gotten into you?"

"I don't know," she replied dully. "I'm terribly sorry."

"You're forgiven," he declared. "But with or without your help, I'm going to get to the bottom of this.

159

And soon. So consider this fair warning. I'm not going to rest until I know *all* the answers."

Julie was relieved to hear the gentleness underlying the steely determination in Garth's voice. Even as she had offered her stilted apology, she had been aware of its inadequacy. She was horrified by the knowledge that he'd spoken the truth. For some reason, when she'd glimpsed his hand coming toward her face she had thought he intended to strike her.

Shortly before one o'clock that afternoon, the mailman delivered a package to Garth, and when Julie took her place at the lunch table a few minutes after the hour, there was a square jeweler's box by her plate. She looked around the table and saw that Garth, Dan, and Jessie were watching her expectantly.

"Is this for me?" she asked.

"Yes," Garth replied evenly. "I telephoned Rupert the other night and asked him to locate it and send it on for you airmail special."

"But why? What is it?"

"Why not open it and find out," Dan said dryly.

Julie fingered the parcel gingerly before she picked it up. As she held it in her palm, she sensed that the others were waiting with bated breath for her to open it. As for her, she felt the same reluctance she'd experienced when Garth had told her to look at the envelope of newspaper articles. She told herself that this time she wouldn't allow herself to indulge in silly forebodings. She squared her shoulders resolutely and without further hesitation she flipped the box open.

After a cursory glance at the ring the box contained, she concentrated on the floral border on her plate. The ring was a marquise-cut yellow diamond in a heavily baroque setting, and she felt an odd aversion to it. Her initial impulse was to simply close the case and cast it away. She looked at the ring again. It was obviously an antique and it occurred to her that Garth might have presented it to her as a wedding or engagement gift; perhaps it was an heirloom that he'd handed down in keeping with family tradition. She forced herself to inspect the ring more closely and grudgingly admitted that, although she would not have chosen the stone or the setting for herself, it was really quite a lovely piece of jewelry.

There was a fine gold chain looped through the band, and the ring slid of its own weight to the center when she lifted it out of the box. She let it swing freely, admiring the way the facets of the jewel trapped the sunlight. The stone sparkled at her. It almost seemed to be winking just at her—as if they were coconspirators—as it spun this way and that on its thin golden chain. It had a mesmerizing effect. Much as she wanted to, she couldn't tear her eyes away from it.

By the time she recognized what was happening to her, before she realized that she could identify the ring and why it was familiar, it was too late.

Time and place began to recede and Julie turned appealingly toward Garth. It was as if she were viewing him through the wrong end of a telescope. He seemed far away—too far away to help her. She was powerless to stem the flow of memories that rushed in. They created an additional obstacle between them, and she sagged into her chair as she shouldered the insupportable burden of the past.

When at last the disorienting feeling began to ebb, she felt the chain cutting into her hand. Automatically she slipped it over her head and the ring dropped inside the open collar of her blouse to settle in an icy weight between her breasts.

"I remember," she said numbly. She moistened her dry lips with the tip of her tongue. "I remember . . . everything." Her lips, her face, all of her, was stiff and cold. She had remembered, and it was not to be borne.

She pushed her chair away from the table so quickly, it fell over with a clatter that brought Buck running from his spot by the living room fireplace. Distressed as she was, Julie recorded this fact, but she did not stop to pat the shepherd, to tell him that she was all right. She was *not* all right.

Garth had risen to his feet, too, and as he followed Julie from the kitchen Jessie suggested uncertainly, "Maybe you'd better let her be by herself for a little while."

He ignored this well intentioned advice and when he heard the front door close behind Julie, he lengthened his stride. Stopping only to grab a couple of coats from the hall closet, he, too, left the house. He kept Julie in sight without attempting to overtake her as she wandered down the lane and crossed the highway to find the path to the river.

She stumbled occasionally as she traversed the rough terrain of the trail, for she walked as if she were in a trance, looking neither to the right nor to the left. It was obvious she was wrestling with a problem so tormenting that she felt compelled to try and run away from it—as she had been, Garth now realized, when she'd left California. He wished she

162

would cry. He wanted to stop her, take her in his arms and tell her to let it all out—all the sorrow, all the fear—but he held himself in check.

His better judgment overruled his desire to shield her from whatever nameless terrors were driving her. For the time being, he didn't think she was prepared to bid farewell to the events of the past that were responsible for her despair. But, Garth thought, when she was ready—this time, please God—he would be there for her.

It was only the river bisecting the trail that stopped Julie's flight. When she reached it, she dropped down to sit on the bank with her legs tucked under her. Garth had thought she was oblivious to his presence, but she wasn't. She had known all along that he was following her.

She touched the scar on her chin. "Had you guessed my grandmother gave me this?" she asked in a cracked whisper. "Is that why you questioned me about it this morning?"

"No, Julie," Garth answered slowly. "I didn't figure that out until I saw the way the ring affected you. Then I noticed how the shape of it matches the scar."

She was holding the stone as if it were some sort of talisman and she visibly relaxed when he made his reply. He moved from his position slightly behind her to sit by her side.

"You knew this was her ring though?"

"Yes, you'd told me it was Elizabeth's. I remarked on the fact that you always wore it and you said it was a keepsake she'd given you."

Julie nodded as he confirmed her recollections. She kept her eyes fixed straight ahead. "I remember," she said tonelessly. "But I didn't tell you she gave it to me as a reminder of a promise I'd made her."

"No, you didn't. I assumed it had come to you after she died."

It was chilly by the river and she was shivering. She let go of the ring to cross her arms over her breasts, and Garth draped the smaller of the jackets over her shoulders before he shrugged into the other one.

"Thank you." She observed the nicety by rote, like a polite child well coached in etiquette. "Would you like me to tell you about it?" she asked.

"Only if you want to."

"I think that you, of all people, are entitled to an explanation."

"Maybe so," he said quietly, "but if that's your only reason for telling me, I'd rather you'd just forget it. Sometimes it's better not to rake over the past."

"No!" she objected adamantly. She turned to look at him, weighing his sincerity. When he risked taking her hand in his, she did not pull away. "I—I want to tell you," she added hesitantly. "I think I *have* to tell you." She briefly returned the pressure of his fingers before she withdrew her hand to touch the mark on her chin.

"This happened when I was fifteen," she said. "We had a terrible row over my plans to go away to school in Eugene, Oregon, where I could get special training in gymnastics."

Garth nodded. "I've heard of the school."

"Looking back, I don't know why I didn't foresee how upsetting this would be to Grandmother." Julie sighed deeply. "I knew she shouldn't become unduly excited. She'd had a stroke about two years before, and her doctor placed special emphasis on the need for her to remain calm."

"The scholarship must have meant a lot to you."

"At the time it meant the whole world. It was my way out. It was a passport to a new life, a different life than the one my grandmother had mapped out for me." Her hand clenched convulsively about the ring. "I was so selfish that I never once stopped to consider how badly this would hurt Grandmother."

"Julie," he reasoned earnestly, "it isn't selfish not to want to walk in someone else's shadow. It's a very natural inclination."

She shook her head doubtfully. "You may be right about that," she admitted, "but once I saw how strenuously she opposed my leaving, I shouldn't have pursued the argument. And I said a terrible thing to her."

Her voice was husky with unshed tears and she cleared her throat before she went on. "Grandmother told me I *couldn't* leave her because I was all she had. And I—I accused her of preferring it that way. I said, 'If you have no one else, it's your own choice.'"

"From what Dan and Jessie have told me about her, it strikes me that you were only speaking the truth."

"True or not, it was very wrong of me to say it," Julie firmly insisted. "Grandmother flew into a rage. She seemed to become a different person and she—she hit me. Twice. Like this." Her hand moved to slap the air in a forceful forehand-backhand gesture. Her voice was barely audible when she continued. "She was wearing the ring—she always did—and the stone caught me on the chin. She'd never struck me before and she couldn't have known how she might injure me."

"I think you're letting her off the hook a little too easily," Garth said grimly.

Julie rushed on as if he hadn't spoken. "When Grandmother saw what she'd done, she looked so very old and she just seemed to—to shrivel. That was when she had her second stroke, and I promised I would never leave her."

"She gave you the ring then?"

"Yes. As a reminder of my promise. As a reminder that I'd given it freely, without her asking me to do so."

"No doubt she intended it as a reminder, but not of any promise you'd made." Garth cupped her cheeks with his hands and turned her to face him. "Oh, honey," he said softly, giving her a little shake, "can't you see that it was supposed to reinforce the guilt you felt because you held yourself accountable for her illness? And needlessly! I mean—my God!— she was in her *seventies*! It could have happened anyway, at any time."

He saw a flicker of uncertainty in the still depths of her eyes. "I'd like to believe you, Garth," she said shakily, "but it happened *then*! And besides, that's not the whole story."

Her throat worked with the sudden sharp stab of remorse that assailed her. Although she described only sketchily her final clash with Elizabeth Ayers, in her imagination she relived each painful detail of the battle.

Elizabeth had always cautioned Julie that the day was bound to come when she would regret being so

166

rebellious. More than once she'd somberly predicted, "If you don't overcome your recalcitrant attitude, young lady, one day you'll go against my wishes once too often. Then you, and you alone, will have to pay the penalty." The severe lines in her face would soften, and she would smile ingratiatingly as she asked, "Do you think I want to see that happen to my own sweet little girl?"

Julie would hang her head and mumble, "No, Grandmother."

She had come to Elizabeth a bewildered not quite five-year-old, and she had learned very quickly that it was forbidden to say anything in praise of her mother or father. As soon as she did, Elizabeth would stop acting the role of doting granny and become stern and cold.

From a very early age Julie had recognized that this giving and withholding of love was a ploy designed to keep her in line, and she'd resented being subjected to it. Yet basically her grandmother was kind to her. Even some of the harshest rules she laid down were for Julie's own good, and if she was possessive and refused to give Julie permission to join in the activities of the other children, it was only because she loved her and was afraid of losing her. After all, as Elizabeth so often pointed out, they had no one but each other.

It was not until she approached her teens that Julie consciously questioned this fundamental premise, around which her grandmother had structured her existence. She began to wonder whether Elizabeth had overprotected her out of a determination to keep her eternally Grandma's own sweet little girl.

As if to prove her surmise, when Julie entered

adolescence and her body started to ripen, Elizabeth sought to instill in her a sense of modesty that approached shame. And when Elizabeth's self-fulfilling prophecy that Julie would eventually defy her once too often came to pass, it seemed inevitable that it should involve a feeble attempt on Julie's part to exercise her newfound maturity by accepting a date with a boy.

The boy in question, Tom Rush, was a year or so older than she. They had several classes together at school and their friendship had blossomed rather tenuously. He asked her out a number of times, but she adhered to her grandmother's interdict and made up excuses for declining his invitations. When he asked her to go to the Junior Prom with him, however, he made it clear that their friendship was at stake.

Julie accepted, for she couldn't bear to nip the fragile bud of affection that had sprung up between them. She had very few friends of her own age and she was lonely. Since her grandmother's last stroke, she had almost no free time. She had to hurry home after school to be with Elizabeth, and her vacations and weekends were occupied with taking care of her grandmother as well, so Julie was unable to participate in ordinary teen-age socializing.

She considered sneaking out to keep her date with Tom, but finally decided against it. It went against the grain not to be forthright, and she wasn't doing anything sinful. When the day of the prom arrived, she explained to Elizabeth, as one adult to another, where she was going that night. On the surface Elizabeth was surprisingly unmoved by the news. The showdown didn't come until Tom brought her home after the dance.

Julie was worried when they drove into the yard and she saw that, with the exception of the porch light, the house was completely dark. She bade Tom a hasty good night and hurried inside. In spite of her concern, she was lighthearted after her innocent evening out and she fairly danced into the parlor.

"Did you have a nice time, dear?" Elizabeth called pleasantly enough from the couch.

As Julie turned on a floor lamp she gaily replied, "I had a wonderful time, Grandmother. But why were you sitting in the dark?"

"I wanted to make sure that boy didn't take any liberties when he brought you home."

"His name is Tom, Grandmother, and he was very gentlemanly." Julie was starry-eyed with pleasure as she held up her wrist to display the silvery little bangle on it. "See," she said softly, "he even gave me a present."

Elizabeth blanched and her eyes hardened. "He *gave* you that?" Her nostrils flared indignantly as she asked, "Are you sure it wasn't payment for services rendered?"

"I—I don't know what you m-mean."

"I think you do!" Elizabeth struggled to her feet and regally drew herself to her full height. "I'd rather see you dead," she hissed, "than have you turn out to be a cheap little tramp like your mother."

Julie counted to ten before she replied and in this way she managed to keep her voice low and steady as she dissented. "My mother wasn't a tramp."

"Oh wasn't she?" A feral glitter entered Elizabeth's eyes. "Then why was she too ashamed to come and see me after she ran off with your good-for-nothing father?"

"Gran," Julie reminded her gently, "you said you'd told her that if she married Daddy, she was no daughter of yours. You *ordered* her to leave and not come back."

"Don't you put words in my mouth, Miss Know-it-all," Elizabeth said scornfully. Her face had grown livid and her breathing was irregular. "If I say your mother was a tramp, it's not half of what she deserves. And you!" she shrieked. "You fall into bed with the first boy who looks at you twice."

"*Please* try not to get excited," Julie begged, her voice rising with concern. "There's no reason for it, because I didn't do anything wrong!"

Elizabeth's breathing was stertorous, and she collapsed onto the couch, lying against the pillows at her back for support.

"I'll get your medicine," Julie cried.

She ran to her grandmother's bedroom to find the mild sedative the doctor had prescribed, and by the time she returned to the parlor Elizabeth was drifting in and out of consciousness. Her flesh seemed to have sunk into her skull and her face was gaunt and ashen. Her lips were blue and she moved them fretfully, trying to speak.

"What is it, Gran?" Julie asked.

Weakly, Elizabeth motioned to her to come nearer and when she did, she reached out to grab her wrist. Her talonlike fingers were astonishingly strong.

"Promise me—" Elizabeth gasped. "Promise—"

"Yes, Grandmother?"

Julie leaned even closer in order to hear what Elizabeth was saying, and a cloud of her grandmother's rose-scented cologne enveloped her in a choking miasma that clogged her nose and throat.

"Swear . . . to me . . . you'll never . . . *never*—"

"I swear it, Gran," Julie blurted hastily.

With a monumental effort Elizabeth pulled herself upright, and her fingers tightened until her nails were digging into Julie's wrist.

"Say it!" she commanded.

Julie knew what Elizabeth was asking of her, and her stomach churned with nausea as she recited the vow her grandmother had so often requested of her. "I swear I'll never leave you, Grandmother."

"And you won't get married!"

"I promise, Grandmother." At that moment Julie would have promised anything to win release so that she could get to the telephone and call the doctor.

Her reserves exhausted, Elizabeth fell back against the upholstery. Her fingers grew limp and she patted Julie's hand approvingly. "You'll always be my own sweet little girl," she muttered raspily. Her eyes rolled wildly, as if she hadn't the strength to coordinate them, and she lost consciousness.

"We never spoke of that night again," Julie said to Garth, "until just before Grandmother died. She must have known she hadn't much longer, because she asked me to repeat my promise to her."

"I can see why you felt obliged to go along with her," Garth remarked, "but you must have recognized that Elizabeth was using emotional blackmail to dictate the way you led your life after she was gone. Surely you never seriously planned to keep your word!"

"No, I don't suppose I ever did. And when I met

you . . . Well, I thought I could handle marriage. Then on the beach that day, you asked about the scar, and it all came back as if it had just happened and I couldn't—" She drew a deep, quivering breath. "It didn't seem right that I should be so happy after what I'd done."

Garth pulled her into his arms and she rested against him gratefully, burying her face in his chest. "It's all right, darling," he said quietly. "I understand."

"Could we visit my grandmother's house before we go home?" she whispered.

"Are you positive you want to?"

Julie nodded emphatically.

Garth's hand moved over her back to the nape of her neck, stopping when it came in contact with the chain. He laced his fingers around her neck as if to assert that his claim on her outweighed Elizabeth's.

He was troubled by her request but he could think of no good reason to deny it. It might even be constructive.

"I don't see why not," he agreed. "When would you like to go?"

"Now!" she exclaimed anxiously. "This afternoon!"

Chapter Thirteen

The house came into view when they reached the brow of the rise. It was smaller than Julie had remembered as it crouched, squat and foursquare, on the hard-packed earth that surrounded it. After today's thaw the yard would be a sea of slick, red mud.

Her grandfather had built the house as a gift for his bride in the early 1930s. With its gables, its broad veranda, and fat round pillars, it tried too hard to be charming and instead seemed merely dated. Probably its original siding had lent it a kind of distinction, but Elizabeth had replaced that with white asbestos shingles many years ago.

It had not fared well in the year it had been vacant. Everything about it showed signs of neglect and abuse. The shrubbery was overgrown, sending out choking tentacles that would screen out most of the light. Most of the windows had been broken and were boarded over, giving the house a blank, aggrieved look, as if it mourned its own demise, and one corner was tilted at an extreme angle, for it was sinking into its cellar. This added to the illusion that it was waiting to pounce on the incautious passerby.

Dan had opposed their coming here. "I don't

think it's a good idea," he'd said, cryptically concise. "It's changed."

Jessie had disagreed. "It's something Julie has to do, Dan," she argued. Dan had looked at her with dismay. "I've made no secret of my feelings about Elizabeth over the years," she'd explained, "so this will probably sound hypocritical, but Julie was the only person who ever loved Elizabeth. For one reason or another, you and a few others may have respected her, but Julie really cared about her. So maybe it's only proper."

Dan was still not convinced of the wisdom of the trip but he offered to call Cal Beatty, the present owner, to clear the visit with him and arrange for him to meet Garth and Julie with the key.

As the sedan bucketed over the rutted surface of the drive, slithering and jouncing with bone-jarring force, Julie saw that Cal had already arrived and was waiting for them in his pickup. Just before they left the drive for the more solid surface of the sparsely graveled barnyard, one of the rear wheels slid into a particularly big pothole, and the car jolted to a stop.

"Damn!" Garth muttered.

He shifted into low gear and rocked the wheel from forward to reverse, trying unsuccessfully to gather sufficient momentum to drive the car out. After several such attempts, he got out to assess the situation. He muttered another oath when he found that the wheel was buried to the middle of the hubcap.

Cal climbed down from the cab of the pickup and came toward them, picking his way with a daintiness that was at odds with his roughcut features and rolling, bowlegged swagger. As he covered the last few steps, he hitched up his trousers and when he reached Garth, he grinned affably and held out his hand.

"You must be Julie's husband," he drawled. "I clean forgot to mention to Dan how bad the road is these days. It hasn't seen a load of gravel for so long, you need four-wheel drive to get over it. I'm surprised you made it this far, but you're sure as hell stuck now!"

"We sure as hell are," Garth ruefully agreed, but he smiled as they shook hands. "Thanks for taking the time to meet us."

"I'm happy to be of service," Cal responded.

Julie got out of the car to join them while they appraised the damage and Cal nodded soberly at her.

"This little lady's always been a favorite of mine," he commented. "It's good to see you, Julie."

"Hello, Cal. How have you been?"

"Can't complain," Cal replied laconically.

He resumed looking down at the wheel, scratching the back of his head as he contemplated it so that his Stetson tilted forward to shade his eyes.

"I have some chain in the truck," he volunteered. "I reckon we can tow it out easy enough."

"I'd appreciate it," said Garth.

"Why don't I unlock the house first so Julie can get a start with whatever it is she wants to do."

As they strolled across the yard, sidestepping the larger mudholes, Cal said, "I'm surely glad you came by, Julie. I've been wantin' to have the house demolished, and the only reason I've held off is 'cause I thought you might want to have one more look around. As you know, most of the furniture's been removed, but there are still some personal things of

175

your grandma's you might want." He shook his head regretfully. "It's gotten to where I have to keep it locked to make sure the kids stay out. It's a real attractive nuisance, and I've been afraid one of 'em would get hurt messin' around inside."

Garth eyed the crazy slope of the partially submerged corner with interest. "Is it safe to go in?" he asked.

"Oh, it's safe enough, all right. Just mind how you go."

When they neared the porch, Cal stopped for a few seconds, standing with arms akimbo as he surveyed the decrepit state of the building. Settling his hat more squarely on his head, he said, "I'm not ashamed to admit this place gives me the creeps. It puts me in mind of a horror movie I once saw. I don't recall the name of it, but Vincent Price was in it."

"House of Usher," Garth provided.

"You saw it too, huh?"

"I read the story," Garth said dryly, "but I see what you mean."

"It's all so dilapidated," Julie observed sadly. "What happened, Cal?"

"Standin' water in the cellar. Bein' deserted. Kids and tramps nosin' around. Besides which, your grandma hadn't done a lick of maintenance for some years."

The floor of the veranda creaked a strident protest as they followed Cal across it. Some of the boards had been torn away, leaving huge gaping holes. Cal pulled a bristling keyring from his coat pocket and, selecting one of the keys, he unlocked the door and swung it open.

"You'll notice I put a deadbolt on," he remarked.

"The old-style locks were so flimsy, it made it too easy to break in."

He moved to one side to allow Julie to step into the house and suggested to Garth, "Let's see about your car now. After I've seen you back to dry land, I won't hang around. Feel free to take your time. I'll come by this evenin' to lock up again."

Garth hung back uncertainly as Cal started down the steps. "I don't know," he said. "I don't like to leave Julie alone—"

"I'll be fine, Garth." She produced a brittle smile. "Honestly I will."

Left with little choice, Garth turned away from her to hurry after Cal's rapidly retreating figure.

Her show of bravery notwithstanding, Julie went into the house with dragging steps. Even though the sun was still far above the horizon, the light in the entry hall was murky. As it always had, the dingy brown wallpaper in the hallway seemed to deaden even the brightest day. The air was cold and dank, and she wrinkled her nose with distaste as she quickly brushed away a cobweb that was sticking to her cheek. The musty odor of mildew, dust, and mice was very strong.

Elizabeth might not have had the ready cash to repair the roof or shore up the foundation or to redecorate the interior, but under her supervision the house had shone with a patina of painstaking attention. It had always been fragrant with a mélange of beeswax, lemon oil, and the potpourri of dried rose petals and spices she had been so fond of.

Julie prowled from room to dismal room, lamenting the extensive signs of malicious destruction. The few remaining pieces of furniture had all been subjected to vandalism of one sort or another. They had broken legs and stained slipcovers; their upholstery was torn and the stuffing was spilling out. She dreaded going into her grandmother's bedroom, and with good reason. When she opened the door and peeked in, she saw that it was the sorriest of all. The wallpaper hung in strips, the ceiling plaster was pocked with holes, and the draperies were in tatters, while the floor was gouged and darkened with scorch marks, as if someone had tried to light a bonfire indoors.

The parlor, on the other hand, had been spared such treatment. Julie avoided this room until she had gone through all the others. It was the one she most associated with her grandmother and even now Elizabeth's presence persisted. She felt it almost tangibly when she entered.

Perhaps the vandals and vagrants had felt it, too, or perhaps they had been dissuaded from coming into the parlor by the portrait of Elizabeth Ayers that guarded the room from its place of honor above the mantel. The portrait had been painted, not too skillfully, by an itinerant artist when Elizabeth was in her late twenties. But while the artist might have had problems with perspective that caused him to render a likeness in which Elizabeth's hair was a shade too red, her lips too thin and her jaw too heavy, he had faithfully captured her eyes and, in them, all the imposing haughtiness of her personality. Her pride, dignity, and iron will seemed to leap from the canvas, empowered by their own vitality.

When Garth returned to the house, Julie was still in the parlor. She was standing by the fine old mantel, staring so intently at Elizabeth's portrait that she didn't notice when he came in. Even when he crossed the room and stood close behind her, she didn't acknowledge him.

He saw that she had pulled the ring outside the collar of her blouse and she was holding it, running the chain through her fingers as if she were saying a rosary. She didn't look at him. She didn't even blink. For a time, he also studied the portrait.

"She was very beautiful," he said at last.

"And very proud." Julie's voice was hushed and without inflection. "I'd forgotten how terribly proud Grandmother was. Maybe that's why I was so frightened by your pride when—"

"What, Julie?" he prompted.

When she did not immediately respond, he put his hands on her shoulders and turned her to face him.

"I do love you, you know," she said in the same apathetic tone. "Those newspaper clippings . . . someone gave them to me just before we left the wedding reception."

Garth's hands tightened on her shoulders. "Charlotte." He spat the name out as if it had left a bad taste in his mouth. "Rupert enclosed a note with the ring to inform me that she'd confessed. According to him, she didn't believe you knew almost nothing about your parents and she wanted to call your bluff. She thought it was a relatively harmless prank to gift wrap the articles and give them to you as a going-away present." He shook his head. "The sad thing is, knowing Charlotte, that's probably the truth!"

Julie's hands worked frantically at her grandmother's ring. "She told me you'd only married me to uphold your family's honor because my father had been blamed for accepting the bribe and your father was instrumental in his conviction. She said you didn't love me, that you never would, that you couldn't love a little nobody like me."

Garth's mouth turned down at the corners. "And you took her word for it?"

"You'd never said you loved me. You still haven't."

"Sometime when you have a few minutes to spare, I'd advise you to read the engraving in your wedding band."

Her hands stilled, and she let go of the chain at her neck to hold her left hand out in front of her, close to Garth's chest. Her eyes shifted incredulously to the wedding band.

"Here," he offered gruffly, taking her hand in his, "let me help you."

Her hand was icy and the ring slipped off her finger easily. He held it so she could see the message that was deeply inscribed inside the band. It read simply FOREVER MY LOVE. Her eyes smarted with tears and she touched the inscription with wonder.

"It's beautiful," she murmured.

Garth cupped the ring in his hand as if he were testing its weight. "I told the jeweler it had to last a lifetime," he revealed. "That's why your ring is so heavy."

"I'm so ashamed—"

Garth placed a silencing fingertip over her mouth. "I *never* want to hear anything further from you about shame or guilt," he instructed firmly. "I think you've had more than your share of that already."

"But I should have had more faith in you."

"The same charge could be leveled at me," he

replied steadily. "As a matter of fact . . ." He drew himself up sharply.

". . . you still have some questions." Julie ended the sentence for him.

He stepped away from her and stood with his hands clasped behind his back, looking up at Elizabeth's portrait.

"You still have to make a choice between your grandmother and me," he said.

"May I have my wedding ring back?" She held out her hand for it.

He turned to confront her. His expression was arrogant as he deliberately slid the ring onto the end of his little finger. It wouldn't go over the first knuckle.

"You can have Elizabeth's ring or mine, but you can't have both. I'll be damned if I'll play second fiddle to a ghost!"

Julie's hand trembled, and her eyes registered her warring emotions. He was suddenly afraid he'd lost his gamble and he moved close to her again.

"I'll even help you make your choice," he said.

Without warning, he grasped the fine gold chain and broke it. It had been accomplished so easily, so quickly, that Julie had had no opportunity to stop him. Her hands darted to catch the ring and chain before they fell to the floor and she held them in her palms, looking at them as if she could not believe the evidence of her own eyes.

"You had no right—"

"I have all the rights I need," he countered sharply. He held up his hand to display the wedding ring. "And this is what gives them to me!"

Julie felt herself wavering and knew how wrong

she had been to return to her grandmother's house. Her choice was clear, not because of the wedding ring but because she loved Garth and she wanted to be with him. Yet something held her back.

Seeing her indecision, Garth put his hand on her shoulder. "Let's go now, darling," he coaxed.

"No!" She shook off his hand. "I—I'm not ready yet. I want to stay just a little while longer."

In the next instant she was swept off her feet when Garth scooped her up in his arms. Grim-faced, he carried her across the room to a sofa that had been overlooked by the vandals in their forays into the house. Without ceremony he dumped her onto it and, sitting beside her, he began pulling off his boots.

She was dazed by the swiftness of his action. "Wha-what are you doing?" she asked.

"What does it look like?" he snapped.

As if to punctuate his question, the boots landed with a thud on the carpet and small puffs of dust rose around them. He peeled off his socks, rolled them into a ball and threw them angrily to the far wall where they rebounded onto the floor. Next, he started to tug his shirttail free of the waistband of his jeans.

"You're going to take off your clothes?" Her voice was shrill. "B-but why?"

"I'm going to exorcise this damned place. For the last time you're going to meet your fear head-on and, once and for all, I'm going to rid you of your grandmother's influence!"

"No! Not here," Julie protested. "Her picture—"

"Is only a picture!"

His eyes blazed like molten steel as he tore his shirt off and tossed it aside. Without pausing, he got to his feet and began to unbuckle his belt and, seeing her chance for escape, Julie rolled off the couch and scurried toward the door. He caught her before she'd taken more than a few steps, his arms clamping around her waist from behind to carry her, kicking and squirming, back to their makeshift bed. When he put her down this time, his attention was diverted to her clothing.

"P-please, Garth," she pleaded, slapping his hands away when he tried to remove her sweater. "I'm so cold."

"If you're patient for just a little while, I'll keep you warm!" He laughed lustily at his own joke, and his eyes glowed with diabolical intent.

"Please!" she repeated, clutching the sweater close to her chin with one hand. A film of tears covered her eyes and blurred Garth's face.

He looked down at her. "All right," he relented, nodding. "You can keep the sweater, but the rest of your things will have to go, so let me have it just for the time being."

Obediently she took the sweater off and handed it to him but she made no move to help him with the rest of her clothes. Garth's chin jutted aggressively, and he began working busily on the row of fastenings on her blouse.

"It's broad daylight," she argued breathlessly.

"You'd never know it by the light in here." He glanced disparagingly around the shadowy room before his eyes returned mercilessly to her. "You'll survive," he said. "Just keep in mind that I won't be seeing anything I haven't seen before." He chuckled humorlessly at her outraged expression and insolently asked, "How do you think I passed the time while

183

I was waiting for you to wake up this morning? You can bet I didn't waste much time contemplating the origin of the universe when I had your heavenly body to contemplate!"

She lay rigidly acquiescent while Garth divested her of her boots, slacks, and blouse, leaving her naked except for abbreviated wisps of underwear. She still held her grandmother's ring clasped in her hand. Her eyes were squeezed shut and although the rest of her face was pinched with cold, her cheeks were bright with embarrassment. Her heart was hammering so hard that the flutter of motion it caused was plainly visible beneath her breast. She felt Garth's hand on her cheek and her eyes flew open.

"You should be proud of your body, Julie," he said softly. "You're very lovely."

Against the rusty black of the couch, her skin lustered alabaster pale and his eyes roamed hotly over her slight form, lingering ardently on the twin mounds of her breasts, her narrow waist, the soft swell of her hips that tapered to slender, sweetly rounded thighs.

Although his hands scalded her when they brushed against her, she made no further attempts to elude him or oppose him as he stripped off her bra and panties. But when he held his hand out for Elizabeth's ring, she clenched it more protectively in her fist and mutely shook her head.

He rose to remove his jeans, and she turned her face toward the back of the couch, refusing to succumb to the temptation to watch him. But nothing could stop her from imagining the way he must look as a faint rustling sound told of his progress.

She could already describe Garth in intimate detail. She knew his body better than she knew her own. Her hands knew the shape of his finely modeled head. Her body knew the length and suppleness of his limbs, the breadth of his shoulders and depth of his chest, the hard strength of his belly and loins, the leanness of his hips. He was totally and devastatingly masculine.

When he lay beside her on the sofa, she kept her face turned away from him.

"My sweater," she reminded him stonily. She made no move to cover herself.

"I'll keep you warm," he repeated with irritating patience. "Anyway, you haven't kept your end of the bargain."

She turned her head to glare at him.

"When you give up the ring," he promised, "you may have your sweater if you want it."

Her lips quivered. "Y-you said you'd never hurt me," she said brokenly. She looked at him accusingly, and he saw the tears that glistened at the tips of her lashes. He sucked in his breath sharply at the sight, hurriedly caught her close, and kissed them away.

"Please, darling." His arms tightened beseechingly. "Try to understand that I only want to set you free."

At first she was cold and so lifeless, she was like a statue in his arms. When she began to thaw in the shared heat of his body, she shivered and her teeth chattered.

Garth was alarmed. She had been so cold that her body's involuntary mechanisms had failed to function and he hadn't even recognized the fact that her temperature had been dangerously low. He tried to disengage his arms from her in order to find something to cover her with, but she murmured protestingly and pressed more closely to him.

As Julie grew warmer, she became fluidly pliant. He began to kiss her lightly and any further resistance was impossible. With her first response, tentative though it was, his mouth became hard and demanding. It was as if he could no longer stave off his desire for her and, infected by his desire, as hungry for him as he was for her, she responded without inhibition to his kisses and caresses, returning them with a passion so volatile, Garth was stunned it could have been contained within her slight body.

When the ring dropped from her relaxed fingers, he cried triumphantly, "Eat your heart out, Elizabeth Ayers." And when Julie laughed at this gibe, Garth knew he had won.

"Are you warm enough?" he asked between kisses. "Do you want your sweater?"

"No," she breathed. Not only was she deliciously warm, she was unable to hold still and she moved constantly, made restless by the intensely pleasurable sensations he was evoking with his questing hands.

"Do you want me to stop?" he whispered against her mouth.

"Don't stop!" So vehement was her denial, her head thrashed from side to side. "I love you. I want you to make love to me."

Garth removed her wedding band from his finger. "Give me your hand," he directed hoarsely. She did so solemnly, and he slipped the ring onto her finger, sealing it in place with a kiss. "With this ring I thee wed," he said. His voice was low and vibrant with emotion. "With my body I thee worship."

She was enthralled by the austere beauty of his face poised above her, and her arms tightened spasmodically around him as she sought the ultimate closeness to him. Sensing her readiness, he molded her to him with his hands urgently on her hips, and she received him gladly. Their bodies meshed, and they came together with an explosive onrush of passion that forged the bond between them and left her gasping, marveling at the rightness of his possession of her.

Their lovemaking was a joyous rededication to their wedding vows, each of them striving to give to the other the supreme pleasure, and their delight was increased beyond measure by the giving. They were willing hostages to their love and for a long time they were drunk with rapture and so blinded by the wonder of fulfillment that they were oblivious to everything but each other.

Reality intruded gradually. Julie became uncomfortably aware that the prickly horsehair fabric that covered the sofa was like sandpaper against the sensitive skin of her back and for the first time Garth realized how chilly it was in the parlor.

When the dustiness of the air in the room made Julie sneeze, he said, "You're cold, darling."

"Not really," she hastily replied. She was reluctant to end their idyll.

But at last, replete with love, they prepared to leave. When they were dressed, Garth leaned over to retrieve Elizabeth's ring from the floor in front of the couch.

"No!" Julie cried. "Leave it!"

He straightened and looked at her quizzically. "Is

there anything else of your grandmother's you'd like to take with you?"

She wandered around the room slowly, pausing to study the portrait. With insight heightened by her love for Garth, she saw that it was only a picture of a discontented young woman who had permitted the insatiable demands of her nature to rule her destiny. In asking too much of others, in giving so little of herself, Elizabeth had willfully planted the seeds of her own unhappiness. She had been doomed to reap the bitter harvest of loneliness she had sown. In no way could her granddaughter be held responsible.

"No," Julie replied quietly. "There's nothing here for me." She looked at Garth and saw that he was frowning. She wished he weren't so far away. "Is something troubling you?" she asked.

A rueful smile erased the frown. "I was just thinking that your loss of memory might have been a stroke of good fortune. Otherwise things might not have ended so happily for us."

"But I'd already discovered I couldn't go through with running away from you!" Julie exclaimed. "Even when I let my grandmother come between us, I think I always knew I had to be with you. That's why I left her ring behind. I'd planned to call you when the bus got into Evanston and tell you—if you still wanted me—that I was coming back! If it hadn't been for the accident—"

"Let's go home, darling," Garth interrupted. He held his hand out to her and his eyes were luminous with tenderness. His smile was jubilant.

She went to him and placed her hand in his. "You're all I'll ever want or need," she said. "Wherever you are *is* home."

Hand in hand, they left the room. Their steps quickened as they crossed the veranda, and they ran with the carefree abandon of children through the yard and down the drive until Julie stopped abruptly. Swinging Garth's hand, she shouted to the hills, "I feel just like Rapunzel! I've been freed from the tower by my handsome prince and I've never been so ha-a-a-appy!"

Laughing, Garth hugged her close to whirl her about in a wild waltz that consumed the remaining distance to the car. They were still laughing and trying to catch their breath when they drove away.

In the parlor of the ranch house a ray from the setting sun penetrated the thicket of branches at the window and glinted on the diamond, causing it to wink and cast a tiny beam of acid-yellow light onto the portrait of Elizabeth Ayers.

If anyone had been there to witness it, they might have thought it resembled a jaundiced teardrop as it lay beneath the inside corner of her eye. And like a tear, it rolled down her cheek as the sun moved lower in the sky and disappeared behind the mountains.

Julie had not looked back.

LOOK FOR NEXT MONTH'S
CANDLELIGHT ECSTASY ROMANCES™:

Love—the way you want it!

Candlelight Romances